LOCKRIDGE

Mikeal Burgin

dizzyemupublishing.com

DIZZY EMU PUBLISHING

1714 N McCadden Place, Hollywood, Los Angeles 90028

dizzyemupublishing.com

Lockridge
Mikeal Burgin

First published in the United States
in 2022 by Dizzy Emu Publishing

1 3 5 7 9 10 8 6 4 2

dizzyemupublishing.com

LOCKRIDGE

Mikeal Burgin

                            LOCKRIDGE

                            Written by

                          Mikeal Burgin

WGAE #I306625

Mikeal Burgin
1202 Palisades Rd
Mount Vernon, IA 52314
(319)775-2889
mikealburgin@gmail.com   WGAE #I306625

TITLE CARD: "Lockridge, Iowa - August 1975"

                                             FADE IN:

1   INT. FARM HOUSE - EARLY MORNING   1

       Alarm clock on the nightstand read 4:29 AM.

       An aging man, HERB SAWYER, sleeps soundly. His dog, GYPSY,
       lies on the floor next to the bed. Alarm clock changes to
       4:30 AM and the alarm sounds.

       Herb stirs and shuts off the alarm clock. Gypsy sits up and
       waits as Herb eases out of bed & grabs his overalls from the
       rocking chair.

2   EXT FARM HOUSE - EARLY MORNING   2

       The SUN is starting to barely rise on the horizon.

       Herb exits the farm house and walks toward the barn, rifle in
       hand, Gypsy follows. A young farmhand, TRAVIS STANLEY, late
       teens/early 20s, exits his pick-up, and walks up the
       driveway.

                         HERB
                   Morning Travis!

       Travis walks past and heads directly toward the barn.

                         TRAVIS
                     (yawning)
                   Morning.

       Herb reaches the parked tractor, and begins to climb in.
       Gypsy turns her attention to the cornfield about 50 yards
       away, she growls & shows her teeth.

                         HERB
                   What's the matter, Gypsy girl? You
                   smell a 'possum?

       Gypsy stands her ground, paying no attention to Herb who
       climbs onto the tractor and fires up the engine.

       Gypsy starts to stalk slowly toward the cornfield. As she
       gets closer, feathers and blood begin to litter the ground.

       Herb throws the tractor headlight on and begins to back up.

Gypsy reaches the edge of the cornfield and holds an aggressive stance, growling loudly. She begins to bark & snarl viciously.

Herb turns to see Gypsy agitated at the corn.

                    HERB (CONT'D)
          Gypsy! C'mon girl!

Gypsy is steadfast on the corn. Really pissed off!

                    HERB (CONT'D)
               (to himself)
          Damn dog! Opossum's playin' dead,
          you ain't scaring it off!

Herb puts the tractor into gear and turns towards Gypsy. As the headlight swings & lights up the cornfield, a long, single monstrous arm flies out of the corn and grabs Gypsy by the neck. She squeals in pain and disappears into the cornfield.

                    HERB (CONT'D)
          GYPSY!

Herb grabs the rifle and dismounts the tractor, running to the corn. Gypsy's squeals continue until a loud snap of her neck is heard and her squealing suddenly stops. Herb arrives and raises the rifle toward the corn, scanning for a sign of it.

                    HERB (CONT'D)
          You son-of-a-bitch! Gimme back my
          dog!

Gypsy's lifeless body flies from the corn and lands next to Herb's feet. Her chest has been ripped open, and field dressed. Herb is shocked at the sight.

                    HERB (CONT'D)
          Gypsy!

A loud sinister purring noise comes from within the corn, it draws Herb's attention and he raises his rifle again.

                    HERB (CONT'D)
          YOU KILLED MY DOG!

Herb fires, a soul shaking roar erupts from the corn, and a huge disturbance explodes from the stalks, knocking Herb to the ground.

Herb struggles to right himself and gather his bearings. Heavy galloping can be heard, growing distant.

The tractor falls to its side in a large crash, as the engine dies and the light goes out.

Travis emerges from the barn and sees the tractor on its side, and Herb stumbling around. He runs toward Herb.

Herb grabs his rifle and turns to aim, he catches a brief glimpse of a large quilled back as it disappears into the forest on the opposite side of his property.

Herb stands and watches the trees, aiming. Travis arrives at his side.

                    TRAVIS
          Are you ok?
                    (beat)
          What the hell was that?

The sun begins to rise behind them, revealing the chaos. Chicken coop has been torn open & ravaged. Wheel of the tractor slowly spins, broken corn stalks splayed out to show multiple chicken carcasses and blood.

                                        FADE OUT.

TITLE CARD: "Present Day"

                                        FADE IN:

3   EXT. MAIN STREET - DAYTIME   3

A car drives past the City of Lockridge sign, leading into town.

Idyllic summer day in the prospering small, quaint town of Lockridge, IA. Citizens walking on main street entering/exiting stores, children riding their bicycles, families engaged.

City Hall is abuzz, many citizens walk in and out of the front doors. A sign in the front window reads: PIPELINE PUMPING STATION - NOW HIRING APPLY TODAY

A small group of Bakken pipeline protesters carrying signs pickets in front of City Hall.

SHERIFF CASEY COLLINS (40s) exits City Hall and makes her way past applicants standing in line. One applicant, JASON EVERS (20s) steps from the line.

                    JASON
          Sheriff...can I ask you a favor?

Sheriff Collins stops. She squints at Jason.

                    SHERIFF COLLINS
          Jason? Is that you?

                    JASON
          Yes ma'am.

                    SHERIFF COLLINS
          You look fantastic! Put on a
          little weight I see.

                    JASON
          Been clean 3 months, 17 days now.

Sheriff Collins smiles.

                    SHERIFF COLLINS
          That is wonderful, good for you!

                    JASON
          Yes ma'am, thank you.

                    SHERIFF COLLINS
          How's Lisa doing?

Jason withdraws a little.

                    JASON
          She's still not good.

                    SHERIFF COLLINS
          I'm sorry to hear that. I hope she
          decides to get herself straightened
          out.

                    JASON
          Yeah...yeah, me too.

                    SHERIFF COLLINS
          So, you wanted to ask me for a
          favor?

                    JASON
          I was wondering if you'd be willing
          to be a reference for me?

                    SHERIFF COLLINS
          You're applying for a job?

Jason fidgets a bit.

                    JASON
          Yes, ma'am.

Sheriff Collins hands Jason her business card.

                    SHERIFF COLLINS
          I'll do what I can to help out.

Jason takes the card and almost breaks down.

                    JASON
          Thank you Sheriff.

Sheriff Collins starts to walk away.

                    SHERIFF COLLINS
          Don't let me down, and stop calling
          me "ma'am." I'm not your mother.

                    JASON
          Yes, ma'am.

Sheriff Collins gives Jason a passing wave as she leaves.

                    SHERIFF COLLINS
          Best of luck on the interview.

Jason puts the business card into the breast pocket of his
dress shirt and gets back in line.

Sheriff Collins walks past the protestors and heads to her
PATROL CRUISER. She spots CLOVER BURESH (50s, good ol' boy)
as she passes and speaks with authority.

                    SHERIFF COLLINS (CONT'D)
          Clover...you stay off the old
          Sawyer property from now on. The
          pumping station is private property
          now.

                    CLOVER
          I'm well within my rights to...

Sheriff Collins interrupts.

                    SHERIFF COLLINS
          You're trespassing, Clover. If I
          catch you out there again you'll be
          spending the night with Sam and
          speaking with Judge Koss in the
          morning.

Sheriff Collins gets into her car and drives away. Clover
scoffs and gets back in the protest line.

4   EXT. CORNFIELD - DAY   4

Rolling cornfields as far as the eye can see. A crew of
DETASSELERS move through the rows.

A young man, CODY PAXTON (15) rummages through the tops of
the stalks. Once he finds one, Cody pulls corn tassels and
drops them on the ground.

Cody moves down the row and suddenly stops. He holds his
hand over his mouth & nose, he retches.

Cody pushes through the stalks, a few rows away is a clearing
of disturbed corn, all laying flat. The sound of flies
buzzing grows louder as he gets closer.

As Cody enters the clearing, the flies are overwhelming as
they swarm around multiple cow carcasses that have been torn
apart.

                         CODY
              Oh my God...

On the opposite side of the clearing is a path that cuts into
the field leading to a heavily wooded area a couple of miles
away.

5   INT. SHERIFF COLLINS CRUISER - DAY   5

Sheriff Collins drives down the highway when her dashboard
computer screen lights up. Sheriff Collins reads the message.

                    SHERIFF COLLINS
              911 Dispatch, report of cattle
              mutilation and possible crop circle
              in Bret Seitzer's cornfield.
              Proceed to County Road Z, mile
              marker 18.

Sheriff Collins slows & turns the cruiser around, heads back
the way she came.

                    SHERIFF COLLINS (CONT'D)
              Well, today just got interesting.

                                                    CUT TO:

6   EXT. MAIN STREET - DAYTIME   6

An open top Jeep pulls into a parking spot out front of City
Hall. CLAYTON SAWYER (mid 30s) climbs out and looks around.

Clayton removes his military jacket and tucks in his shirt
in, checks his face in the side mirror. He heads toward the
front door of City Hall.

7   INT. CITY HALL - DAYTIME   7

CITIZENS stand in line against the wall in a hallway,
clipboards in hand, filling out paperwork.

HARRIET THURMAN stands at the counter, speaking to a young
woman and pointing at her application. The woman signs the
application and turns to leave. Harriet calls toward the
line without looking.

                         HARRIET
                    Next...

Clayton approaches the table, military pack over his
shoulder, dog tags around his neck. Harriet looks up and
immediately recognizes Clayton.

                         HARRIET (CONT'D)
                    Dear Lord...Clayton Sawyer! How
                    have you been? It's fantastic to
                    see you back.

                         CLAYTON
                    Hey Harriet, it's good to see you
                    too.

                         HARRIET
                    Heavens, you sure look good! How
                    long's it been now?

                         CLAYTON
                    13 years...I've been gone 13 years.

                         HARRIET
                    Good lord, it seems twice that!
                    We're all real proud of you around
                    town. Regular American hero! Your
                    Dad kept us updated on all the
                    details.

                         CLAYTON
                    I bet he did.

                         HARRIET
                    I'm so sorry about your father,
                    hon'. He was a good, honest man.
                    His funeral was gorgeous.

                    CLAYTON
          Yeah, that's what I heard.

                    HARRIET
          So, Mayor said you would be
          stopping by soon. Wanted me to
          give this to you.

Harriet hands Clayton an envelope. He opens it, a check from
ALLIED ENERGY ASSOCIATES for the amount of $200,000 is
inside.

                    CLAYTON
          Thank you.

                    HARRIET
          Have you been out to your old place
          yet?

                    CLAYTON
          Nope, not yet.

                    HARRIET
          Well, you should give it a few
          days. So many changes since you
          were last here, don't over do it.

                    CLAYTON
          It's ok, Harriet. I heard the
          house & farm are all gone.

Harriet reaches out and touches Clayton's arm.

                    HARRIET
          I'm sorry, hon'. Mayor Stanley
          pushed through that eminent domain
          paperwork on your property so fast,
          nobody in the county even knew it
          happened until it was already
          approved.

Clayton nods.

                    CLAYTON
          So is Travis in? I need to speak
          to him.

                    HARRIET
          No, he's not at the moment, and
          he'll give you an earful if you
          don't address him as "Mayor." He's
          helping the oil folks do interviews
          for the pumping station.
                    (MORE)

                    HARRIET (CONT'D)
          Might be a day or two, most
          everyone in town is applying for
          jobs. Are you in town for long?

                    CLAYTON
          I'll be around for a few days.

                    HARRIET
          Well, you just keep checking back
          in, and I'll tell him you were
          here.

                    CLAYTON
          Sounds good.

                    HARRIET
          You take care now, Clayton.

Clayton turns to leave, Harriet turns her attention back to
the line of applicants.

                    HARRIET (CONT'D)
          Next.

8   INT. CITY HALL - DAYTIME   8

Clayton exits the conference room and walks down the hallway
toward the front door. 2 HUNTERS stand at a side counter and
turn to leave, each holding their new hunting license, and
nearly run into Clayton.

                    HUNTER 1
          Sorry buddy.

                    CLAYTON
          No problem.

                    HUNTER 2
          Hey, you're local, huh? Where are
          the best hunting spots around here?

                    CLAYTON
          In Lockridge?

Both hunters wait with anticipation.

                    CLAYTON (CONT'D)
          About 50 miles south in Keokuk.

Clayton walks away without saying another word. Both hunters
balk at his response and retreat in the opposite direction.

9   EXT. CORNFIELD - DAY   9

Sheriff Collins stands in the clearing, she swats at flies as
multiple detasselers line the edge of the clearing, some
recording with their cell phones.

Sheriff Collins speaks into her shoulder-mounted radio.

                    SHERIFF COLLINS
          Dispatch, call Kent Barker and let
          him know we found his missing
          cattle, all deceased.

                    DISPATCHER
               (over radio)
          Roger that.

Cody approaches Sheriff Collins cautiously.

                    CODY
          Hey Sheriff, you think it's aliens?

Sheriff Collins grins.

                    SHERIFF COLLINS
          Not hardly, coyotes would be more
          like it.

Sheriff Collins squats down to point out paw prints all
around the area.

                    SHERIFF COLLINS (CONT'D)
          See, coyotes.

                    CODY
          Never seen coyotes take down a herd
          of cattle.

Sheriff Collins stands back up and advances further into the
clearing.

                    SHERIFF COLLINS
          I wouldn't call this much of a crop
          circle either. Looks like the cows
          were herded, or chased, from there.

Sheriff Collins gestures toward the path leading into the
clearing.

DETASSELER #1 calls out from the edge of the clearing.

                    DETASSELER #1
          SHERIFF! I found something!

Detasselers crowd around Detasseler #1 as Sheriff Collins approaches slowly. Detasselers film the find with their cell phones as Sheriff Collins pushes her way through and takes a look.

A long marbleized shaft with a barbed point is sticking out from underneath one of the carcasses.

> CODY
> What is it?

> SHERIFF COLLINS
> I'm not sure.

Sheriff Collins pulls the shaft out from underneath the cow, several feet of shaft are withdrawn. Sheriff Collins holds it up and examines it closely.

> SHERIFF COLLINS (CONT'D)
> Looks like a quill.

> CODY
> That's definitely aliens!

Sheriff Collins gives Cody a "look".

> SHERIFF COLLINS
> Probably from a feather that's been
> stripped. Coyotes probably came
> back and got hold of a turkey
> vulture that was feeding on the
> carcasses.

Sheriff Collins hands the quill to Cody.

> CODY
> Stupid feather!

Cody turns and javelin throws the quill into the cornfield. Sheriff Collins speaks into her shoulder radio again.

> SHERIFF COLLINS
> Dispatch, I'm closing the case on
> this one. Nothing more than a
> coyote attack, tell Kent Barker to
> keep his cattle in at night for a
> while. I'm going to call it a day,
> I'll write up the report tomorrow
> morning.

> DISPATCHER
> 10-4.

Sheriff Collins exits the clearing as detasselers are taking
selfies with the carcasses.

10   INT. PUMPING STATION CONTROL ROOM - DUSK   10

2 EMPLOYEES sit at a control board. Employee 1 types on his
computer, while Employee 2 writes down data being read from
mounted gauges.

Employee 1 stretches in his chair, stands and walks to a
coffee machine across the room. He pours himself a cup and
stares out the window while he takes a sip.

11   EXT. PUMPING STATION YARD - DUSK   11

Employee 1 gazes out the window, the sun is setting.
Suddenly a massive herd of deer come charging across the yard
from the direction of the forest, dodging between generators
& mounted vents.

12   INT. PUMPING STATION CONTROL ROOM - DUSK   12

Employee 1 turns to Employee 2

                    EMPLOYEE 1
          Hey, check this out. Huge herd of
          deer on the run!

Employee 2 darts over to the window to see.

                    EMPLOYEE 2
          Holy shit! Look at 'em all!

                    EMPLOYEE 1
          Check out the buck!

                    EMPLOYEE 2
          Gotta be a 14 point easily! Would
          love to have that rack mounted at
          home!

A large disturbance is heard outside, away from the employees
view.

                    EMPLOYEE 1
          What the hell was that?

Both Employees struggle to see what caused the noise. A loud
beeping starts to emit from the control panel and draws
Employee 2's attention.

He approaches the control panel, studies the screen, & shuts off the noise by pushing a button.

                    EMPLOYEE 1 (CONT'D)
          Shit! We got another pump down!

                    EMPLOYEE 2
          Again? That's the third one this
          week!

                    EMPLOYEE 1
          Yeah, and it's your turn too! #7
          this time.

Employee 2 grabs a large flashlight.

                    EMPLOYEE 2
          Probably just one of the deer ran
          into a generator and dislodged the
          power source. Be right back.

Employee 2 exits the room. Employee 1 continues to watch out the window.

13   EXT. PUMPING STATION YARD -EVENING   13

Employee 2 exits the main control room building and walks across the yard. He looks up at Employee 1 in the window and flips him the finger. Employee 1 points in the direction of the pump and Employee 2 shakes his head reluctantly.

                    EMPLOYEE 2
          Yeah, yeah...I'm going, Dickhead!

14   INT. PUMPING STATION CONTROL ROOM - EVENING   14

Employee 1 watches as Employee 2 walks across the yard, and disappears from sight. Employee 1 walks back over to his desk and watches a bank of security cameras. Employee 2 walks into frame.

15   EXT. PUMPING STATION YARD - EVENING   15

Employee 2 reaches pump #7, shines his flashlight at it. The pump is completely crushed in on one side, a small pillar of smoke rises from it, and a distinct buzzing noise can be heard rising from inside. He pans his light around the area, there is a dead doe laying about 30 feet away, her neck twisted, her head facing backward over her shoulders.

                         EMPLOYEE 2
                    Stupid deer!

Employee 2 motions at the security camera and shows 7
fingers, and then gives the "throat cut" signal.

16   INT. PUMPING STATION CONTROL ROOM - EVENING   16

Employee 1 watches Employee 2, and cuts power to pump #7.

17   EXT. PUMPING STATION YARD - EVENING   17

The buzzing slowly fizzles out. Employee 2 walks over to the
doe.

                         EMPLOYEE 2
                Not gonna let the meat go to waste!

He grabs the doe by the hind leg and starts to drag it back
the way he came.

Across the yard behind Employee 2 a loud grunt is heard,
followed by a guttural purring. Employee 2 spins around
quickly and shines his light in that direction.

The light barely has the power to scan the treeline.
Employee 2 takes a couple of steps toward it, searching.

18   INT. PUMPING STATION CONTROL ROOM - EVENING   18

Employee 1 watches Employee 2 on the screen as he disappears
from the camera view.

                         EMPLOYEE 1
                What the hell are you doing now?

19   EXT. PUMPING STATION YARD - EVENING   19

Employee 2 scans the treeline with his light. The purring
starts again, and he shines the light in its direction.

There is a slight swaying within the forest. Slowly two
large gray balls of light appear to open while the light
shines on them. They blink.

                         EMPLOYEE 2
                    What the hell?

The swaying intensifies as a bellowing roar comes from the
trees. Employee 2 falls to the ground.

Something bursts from the treeline and charges. Employee 2 scrambles to get up, thunderous galloping & heavy guttural breathing coming up fast behind him, he begins to run.

20   INT. PUMPING STATION CONTROL ROOM - EVENING   20

Employee 1 can see some sort of commotion just off screen, hurried shadows, scattered light.

21   EXT. PUMPING STATION YARD - EVENING   21

Employee 2 runs, the dead doe is on the ground in front of him. He jumps to clear it.

22   INT. PUMPING STATION CONTROL ROOM - EVENING   22

Employee 2 enters frame by leaping over the doe, and is yanked back violently out of mid air.

                    EMPLOYEE 1
             What in the Sam hell was that?

The screen is still. Employee 1 watches closely. Employee 2's body is tossed across the yard and lands on the other side of the dead doe.

                    EMPLOYEE 1 (CONT'D)
          HOLY SHIT!

Employee 1 watches the screen. The eye shine from the creature looms in the darkness just barely on screen. Swaying quills tower above it, in the light of the station. Something emerges quickly from the dark, grabs the doe, and retreats.

Employee 1 jumps across the room, picks up the phone and dials.

                                        CUT TO:

23   INT. CHILD'S BEDROOM - NIGHT   23

JAKE COLLINS (40s) sits on the bed of his daughter, SADIE COLLINS (10-14, with down syndrome), reading a story to her who watches the book intently.

Sheriff Collins enters the room, tucking her uniform into her jeans.

                    SHERIFF COLLINS
          Call just came in, there was some
          sort of attack at the pumping
          station. I'll be back as soon as I
          can.

Jake stops reading, Sadie sits up.

                    JAKE
          Attack?

                    SHERIFF COLLINS
          Yeah, sounds like some sort of
          animal had a go with one of the
          overnight employees.

                    JAKE
          Animal?

                    SHERIFF COLLINS
          Well, coyotes are thick this year.
          They're all competing for food, so
          run-ins with people are more
          common.

Sadie is concerned.

                    SADIE
          Don't let coyotes get you too
          mommy!

Casey enters the room and plants a kiss on Sadie's forehead.

                    SHERIFF COLLINS
          No way, kiddo! I'm the only
          vicious animal in this county!

Sadie wraps her arms around Casey's neck.

                    SADIE
          I love you, mommy!

                    SHERIFF COLLINS
          Love you too, Sadie.

Sadie lets go and lies back down. Casey leans in to Jake.

                    SHERIFF COLLINS (CONT'D)
          I'm sorry. I'll be back soon.

                    JAKE
          Yeah, right...I'll see you in the
          morning if I'm lucky.

Casey kisses Jake.

> SHERIFF COLLINS
> If you're lucky I'll make it up to
> you at the same time!

Jake raises his eyebrows in approval. Casey heads towards
the door.

> JAKE
> Be safe, love you.

> SHERIFF COLLINS
> Always am, love you too.

Casey leaves and Jake continues reading.

24   EXT. SHERIFF COLLINS HOME - NIGHT   24

Something drags the dead doe by a leg through the woods. It
notices a clearing. A two story country home is illuminated
both inside & out.

Sheriff Collins exits the front door of the home and enters
her cruiser. She turns the engine over and drives away
quickly.

Something watches from the treeline.

25   INT. CHILD'S BEDROOM - NIGHT   25

Jake finishes the book.

> JAKE
> ...and they lived happily ever
> after. The end.

Jake looks down and Sadie has fallen asleep. Jake gets up
slowly, tucks Sadie in, turns off the room's light, and shuts
the door behind him.

26   EXT. SHERIFF COLLINS HOME - NIGHT   26

Something watches as the light in the house turns off.
Curiosity pulls something from the trees into the open yard.

27   INT. CHILD'S BEDROOM - NIGHT   27

Sadie sleeps, the room is illuminated by a night light under
the window next to Sadie's bed.

The light of the moon outside is slowly obscured by a solid
silhouette of something outside the window. It tilts its
head to look around the room inside. Heavy breathing is
heard, which turns into a guttural purring.

Sadie slowly wakes from the noise and sits up in bed. She
tilts her head toward the window and sees the eye shine,
watching her.

Sadie is timid, but watches something watch her. She reaches
up to the window with her hand. Something drops the doe and
reaches to the window. A distant howl pulls something's
attention, and it withdraws and heads toward the howl. Sadie
jumps from bed and looks out the window.

                                             CUT TO:

28   EXT. PUMPING STATION YARD - NIGHT   28

Sheriff Collins pulls up to the crime scene in her cruiser.
There is another car there already, the crime scene has been
taped off, and Highway Patrolman SAM MOORE is covering the
body with a sheet.

Sheriff Collins exits the car and approaches.

                         SAM
                Sheriff...

                         SHERIFF COLLINS
                What happened Sam?

                         SAM
                One dead employee, and I mean
                REALLY dead. Other employee claims
                it was an animal of some sort,
                something big, but claims he
                couldn't see it.

                         SHERIFF COLLINS
                So how does he know it was
                something big?

                         SAM
                Because it threw the victim.

                         SHERIFF COLLINS
                Threw him?

                         SAM
                Uh huh!

Casey lifts the sheet. Employee 2's skull is crushed.
Sheriff Collins puts the sheet back down in disgust.

                    SHERIFF COLLINS
          This doesn't look like an animal
          attack.

                    SAM
          That's what I thought too. It's
          blunt force trauma, right? But
          then I saw this.

Sam shines his large MAG-LITE on the ground. An enormous
bloody knuckle print is on the concrete.

                    SHERIFF COLLINS
          What is that?

                    SAM
          No idea! But it's huge, what ever
          it is! We're transferring the
          digital surveillance video of the
          whole thing to see what we can make
          out.

Sheriff Collins takes the Mag-Lite from Sam and shines it
across the yard, following the trail. It leads into the
forest.

                    SHERIFF COLLINS
          Better call Fairfield, and let's
          get the video queued up back at the
          station as soon as possible. Mayor
          Stanley will want to see it in the
          morning.

Sam nods and retreats back to his car.

29   EXT. WOODED CAMPSITE - NIGHT   29

Hunter 1 & 2 celebrate around a campfire, empty beer cans
litter the campsite, 3 dead coyotes hang from a tree.

                    HUNTER 2
          The last one just stood there in
          the spotlight next to his mate and
          howled before you blasted it! How,
          how, HOWWWWWWWWLLLLLLed!

                    HUNTER 1
               (laughing)
          50 miles south my ass!

> HUNTER 2
> (giggling)
> Plenty of stupid animals here to
> move closer to extinction!

Hunter 1 raises his arms as if he's aiming a rifle and mimics
shooting.

> HUNTER 1
> All in the name of conservation!

Both hunters burst into laughter.

30   EXT. WOODS - NIGHT   30

Something stalks toward the hunters' campsite, obscured by a
large tree. It spots the coyote carcasses, and grunts its
approval.

31   EXT. WOODED CAMPSITE - NIGHT   31

A thunderous grunt bellows close. Both hunters snap to
attention.

> HUNTER 1
> What the fuck was that?

Hunter 2 scrambles for his gun.

> HUNTER 2
> A bear maybe?

> HUNTER 1
> There's no bears in Iowa, dumbass!

Hunter 2 points his gun toward the large tree. There appears
to be something swaying behind it, on both sides, about 8
feet off the ground

> HUNTER 2
> It's moving! Get the light!

Hunter 1 reaches down next to his folding chair to grab a
searchlight. Something growls its displeasure, and startles
Hunter 1.

> HUNTER 2 (CONT'D)
> Will you hurry up?!

A quick commotion from the tree draws the hunters' attention
back. Hunter 1 turns the spotlight on the tree, there is
nothing there.

                    HUNTER 2 (CONT'D)
          Go check it out, I'll cover you.

Hunter 1 draws a large buck knife from his belt and shines
the light forward as he approaches the tree cautiously. He
rounds the tree and scans the light deeper into the forest.
Something has disappeared.

                    HUNTER 1
          It's gone!

Something reaches down from up in the tree and grabs Hunter 1
by the head, lifting him 6 feet off the ground. Something
gives Hunter 1's head a quick twist and snaps his neck like a
twig. Hunter 1 drops the spotlight and it shuts off, the
woods go dark again.

There is a large thud on the ground by the tree followed by
staggered galloping around the campsite. Hunter 2 is firing
his rifle over and over again until he runs out of bullets.

Hunter 2 searches his pockets for more bullets, he finds
none. A deep growl comes from behind Hunter 2 who spins
around and falls backwards. Eye shine from something glows
orange from the dark behind the campfire.

Hunter 2 starts to crawl backwards toward the large tree.
Heavy footsteps and purring are heard as something draws
closer to the fire. Something lifts Hunter 1 up by his head,
his limp body dangles like a marionette. Something crushes
Hunter 1's head with his enormous hand and it explodes like
squeezing an egg. Hunter 1 crumples to the ground in a heap.

                    HUNTER 2
          Please God, please!

Hunter 2 pulls out his cell phone and dials 911. Ringing is
heard as Something reaches down and picks up a huge rock from
the fire pit circle, and throws it at Hunter 2, striking him
in the chest and throwing him back against the large tree.
The phone is answered

                    911 OPERATOR
          911, what is your emergency?

Something roars, grabs the 3 coyotes from the tree and
disappears into the darkness of the woods.

32   EXT. PUMPING STATION YARD - NIGHT   32

Sam speaks into the CB inside his cruiser as headlights
approach him from behind. Sam turns to see who it is.

Clayton's Jeep pulls to a stop to the rear of the cruiser.
Clayton sits in his Jeep taking in the situation going on
around him.

Sam returns the CB and approaches Clayton's Jeep.

                    SAM
          Clayton.

                    CLAYTON
          Hey, Sam.

                    SAM
          Been a while.

                    CLAYTON
          Yeah.

                    SAM
          When'd you get back in?

                    CLAYTON
          Today.

Clayton leans forward, see's Sheriff Collins standing over a
sheet as she talks to Employee 1.

                    CLAYTON (CONT'D)
          What's happened here, Sam?

Sam looks in the same direction as Clayton.

                    SAM
          Industrial accident.

Clayton starts to scan the woods surrounding the property.

                    SAM (CONT'D)
          Anyway, this property ain't none of
          your business anymore, Clayton.
          Mind telling me what you're doing
          here?

                    CLAYTON
          I, uh, wanted to see what they've
          done with the place.

Sam looks in the back of Clayton's Jeep, he lifts his
flashlight and illuminates a few dead raccoons & opossums.

                    SAM
          You got a permit for all of these?

                    CLAYTON
          Don't need one. Road kill.

                    SAM
          Road kill, huh?

Clayton continues to physically ignore Sam, looking around
the property. Sam considers the situation.

                    SAM (CONT'D)
          Is that marijuana I smell?

This pulls Clayton's attention back.

                    CLAYTON
               What?

                    SAM
          You been out celebrating your
          return to Lockridge? Make it a bit
          easier for you to see the old
          homestead ripped apart?

Sam's demeanor changes, he leans in close to Clayton.

                    SAM (CONT'D)
          This isn't the Middle East, back
          here you're just a citizen like
          everyone else. I'm the only hero
          in Jefferson county! Don't you
          forget that!

Sheriff Collins steps up behind Sam and interrupts.

                    SHERIFF COLLINS
          Good evening, Clayton.

Sam rights himself, and stares Clayton down as he steps back
from the Jeep and stands slightly in front of Sheriff
Collins.

                    CLAYTON
               Sheriff.

                    SHERIFF COLLINS
          We have a pretty bad accident here.

                    CLAYTON
               Yeah?

Sam answers.

                    SAM
          I think he's on something, Sheriff.
          He's got a bunch of dead animals in
          the back.

Sheriff Collins tries to step around Sam to have a look. Sam
steps back in front of her, cutting her off.

                    SAM (CONT'D)
          He won't look me in the eye and I
          smell marijuana. I was just about
          to search the vehicle and take him
          in.

                    SHERIFF COLLINS
          Nonsense, you're doing nothing of
          the sort.

Sam grinds his teeth and steps aside. Sheriff Collins moves
in closer to Clayton. Sam exits and heads toward Employee 1.

                    SHERIFF COLLINS (CONT'D)
          So what's your business out here,
          Clayton?

                    CLAYTON
          Like I told Sam, I wanted to see
          what has changed around the
          property.

Clayton begins looking around the property. Sheriff Collins
looks back at the crime scene before looking back at Clayton.

                    SHERIFF COLLINS
          Well, you already know the whole
          thing has changed. The oil company
          doesn't want anyone on this land,
          especially with all of the
          protests.

Clayton doesn't appear to find what he's looking for, and
gives Sheriff Collins his undivided attention. Sam escorts
Employee 1 to his car, and he drives away as Sam rejoins
Sheriff Collins.

                    CLAYTON
          Yes ma'am.

                    SHERIFF COLLINS
          Now, what's with all the animals?

Clayton turns to look in his backseat.

                    CLAYTON
          Nothing, just cleaning up the
          roadways a little.

                    SHERIFF COLLINS
          You doing ok?

Clayton looks at Sheriff Collins oddly.

                    CLAYTON
          What do you mean?

Sam interrupts from behind Sheriff Collins.

                    SAM
          She means has the war gotten into
          your head a little bit? Maybe it's
          got your foot on the gas, but
          nobody's steering anymore?

Clayton glares at Sam.

                    SHERIFF COLLINS
          What I'm saying is that in all my
          years as Sheriff of this county,
          I've seen quite a few crazy things,
          but I've never seen someone
          purposely picking up back highway
          road kill and hauling it around in
          their vehicle. Then showing up at
          what is being considered a crime
          scene. It all looks pretty...

Clayton interrupts her.

                    CLAYTON
          Suspicious?

                    SHERIFF COLLINS
          I was going to say odd. This isn't
          like the Clayton Sawyer I knew.

Clayton is silently defiant. A WHITE VAN pulls into the
property behind the gathering, Sam steps back and waves it
around. The white van drives past, the side wall reads
FAIRFIELD CITY CORONER.

                    SHERIFF COLLINS (CONT'D)
          Now there's no crime in doing what
          you're doing, but I'm just
          concerned as to why you're doing
          it.

                    CLAYTON
          I'm fine, Sheriff.

A call from the DISPATCHER comes across the Sheriff's CB.
Sam opens the door to the cruiser and answers.

                    SAM
          Sam here, go ahead dispatch.

                    DISPATCHER
          911 call a little while ago, took
          us a while to trace it. Coming from
          somewhere around tower 3, about 6
          miles from where you are.

                    SAM
          Dispatch, that's a completely
          wooded area, what is the nature of
          the call.

                    DISPATCHER
          We're not sure. There was a lot of
          screaming & commotion, and then it
          all suddenly stopped, but nobody
          ever hung up the phone. They're
          still there even now.

                    SAM
          10-4 we're en route.

Sam whistles at Sheriff Collins.

                    SAM (CONT'D)
          Dispatch has another call, could be
          related, we gotta go!

Sheriff Collins nods in agreement and then turns back to
Clayton.

                    SHERIFF COLLINS
          I don't want to see you out here
          anymore, understand?

Clayton is unsettled by what Sam has said.

                    SHERIFF COLLINS (CONT'D)
          Take care of yourself, Clayton.

Sheriff hands Clayton his keys back, then removes herself and
hops into her cruiser as Sam takes off quickly down the
driveway. Sheriff Collins turns her cruiser around quickly
and follows.

Clayton starts his engine, he sits in his car for a moment and watches as sirens ignite the highway in a flood of red & blue.

                         CLAYTON
               God damn it, Clayton!

Clayton throws the Jeep into gear and whips around. He follows the same route that the Sheriff & Sam took.

33   EXT. ROADSIDE - NIGHT   33

Sheriff Collins & Sam pull up their cruisers next to a large pick-up truck, with license plates that read SHOOTEM, parked along a desolate 2 lane highway. Sheriff Collins is the first to exit her vehicle, with a hand on her firearm. She walks to Sam's vehicle. Sam exits his cruiser with a shotgun.

                         SHERIFF COLLINS
               This has got to be it.

Sam scans the side of the road, an empty beer can lays on the ground just a few feet from the treeline.

                         SAM
               After you, Sheriff.

Sam hands the Mag-Lite to Sheriff Collins, then pumps the action on his shotgun. Sheriff Collins removes her gun from its holster.

                         SHERIFF COLLINS
               Stay close.

Sheriff Collins crosses in front of the pick-up truck, Sam follows. They cautiously enter the woods, the light from Sam's Mag-Lite illuminates the interior of the trees as they proceed further.

34   INT. WOODS - NIGHT   34

Sheriff Collins shines the light back & forth, as they continue to walk, both with their gun barrels leading the way.

There is a flash of light further into the woods as Sheriff Collins scans.

                         SAM
               What was that?

Sheriff Collins scans back and fixes the Mag-Lite beam on the
glow in the woods.

                    SAM (CONT'D)
          That's eye shine!

Sheriff Collins motions for Sam to flank left so they can
both approach from different directions.

As Sheriff Collins approaches, and rounds the corner of the
trees, more eyes begin to shine. From 15 feet away she
begins to recognize what she is finally seeing, a mass of fur
& blood. 3 dead coyotes have been mangled, not much left
except for heads.

Sam walks in silently from the opposite side.

                    SAM (CONT'D)
          Dear God!

Sheriff Collins squats down for a closer look.

                    SHERIFF COLLINS
          I've only got 3 heads. Coyotes.

                    SAM
          What's happened to them?

Sheriff Collins examines further.

                    SHERIFF COLLINS
          This one's ribs are completely
          crushed, and its skin is ripped.
          Like someone tore a piece of paper
          in half. Looks like they've
          been...eaten.

                    SAM
          Eaten?

Sheriff Collins notices another light further back in the
woods. She points it out to Sam.

                    SHERIFF COLLINS
          There!

Sam nods and they slowly head towards the light with Sam
circling around wider from Sheriff Collins.

35   EXT. WOODED CAMPSITE - NIGHT   35

Sheriff Collins & Sam enter the hunters' campsite from
opposite sides.

It is destroyed, Hunter 2 is leaning against a tree, Sam
bends down to check his pulse and then gives up when he
notices the boulder embedded in his chest.

                    SAM
          I've got 1 dead over here.

Sheriff Collins stands above the headless body of Hunter 1,
her face is flush & pale.

                    SHERIFF COLLINS
          There's another over here.

Sam scans around the outlying woods with his shotgun.
Sheriff Collins looks down next to Hunter 1's corpse, in the
dirt & blood mixture of the ground, there is the distinct
impression of knuckle prints, same as from the pumping
station.

                    SHERIFF COLLINS (CONT'D)
          Sam, I don't think we've got the
          manpower to handle this situation.
          I'm thinking we need to get back to
          the cruiser and call Fairfield for
          back-up. Maybe they can get a
          chopper out here with thermal
          imaging.

Sam backs up next to Sheriff Collins.

                    SAM
          What's the matter? You scared,
          Little Lady?

Sheriff Collins turns to leave the campsite, Sam follows as a
figure bursts through the woods right in front of Sheriff
Collins & Sam. Both point their weapons at it.

                    CLAYTON
          Wait, wait, wait! Don't shoot!
          It's me!

Sheriff Collins lowers her weapon, Sam keeps his on Clayton.

                    SHERIFF COLLINS
          You have got some serious
          explaining to do, Clayton.

                    CLAYTON
          I know...I should have told you
          back at the pumping station.

                    SAM
          Told us what?

                    CLAYTON
          I know what's killing these people.

Sam continues to hold him in his sights.

                    SAM
          Just give me one good reason...

Sheriff Collins flashes Sam a look. Sheriff Collins removes
her hand cuffs and approaches Clayton.

                    SHERIFF COLLINS
          Turn around and put your hands
          behind your back!

Clayton follows the orders without resistance. Sheriff
Collins secures Clayton's wrists, and gives him a nudge back
toward the way they came.

                    SHERIFF COLLINS (CONT'D)
          Let's go!

All three exit the campsite.

36   INT. LOCKRIDGE POLICE DEPT. - NIGHT   36

Clayton sits at an empty table, still handcuffed, in a small
interrogation room.

Sheriff Collins enters the room with a bottle of water and
removes the handcuffs. Clayton rubs his wrists while Sheriff
Collins sits at the table opposite him.

                    SHERIFF COLLINS
          OK, tell me about what you were
          saying at the campsite.

Clayton struggles to find a place to start.

                    SHERIFF COLLINS (CONT'D)
          The level of seriousness here is
          monumental, so you need to start
          explaining to me what you know
          about tonight.

                    CLAYTON
          You know, it's funny, but I've had
          moments where I've had to tell the
          rest of my platoon that one of our
          own had died in the line of duty.
          Compared to what I'm about to tell
          you, those conversations seem
          trivial by comparison.

Sheriff Collins slides the bottle of water across the table
to Clayton. He opens it and takes a drink.

                    SHERIFF COLLINS
          Clayton...did you kill those people
          tonight?

                    CLAYTON
          Do you see any blood on me?

                    SHERIFF COLLINS
          You've put yourself at the scene of
          3 deaths this evening, Clayton.
          Blood or not, I need to know why
          you're not the suspect.

                    CLAYTON
          I was hoping to talk to the Mayor
          today. I'm not here to just pick
          up my check from the sale of the
          land.

                    SHERIFF COLLINS
          What are you here for then?

                    CLAYTON
          He made a mistake selling my land,
          and I came here to stop it.

                    SHERIFF COLLINS
          The station is already operational,
          Clayton.

                    CLAYTON
          No, not that. It's about what my
          grandfather saw on the farm all
          those years ago.

Sheriff Collins is trying to comprehend what he just said.

                    SHERIFF COLLINS
          The monster sighting?

Clayton looks away from Sheriff Collins, nodding.

                    SHERIFF COLLINS (CONT'D)
          You're trying to tell me that a
          monster killed those people?

Clayton senses the condescension, but eventually nods again.

                    SHERIFF COLLINS (CONT'D)
I'm at a bit of a loss here,
Clayton. Now I am starting to get
a bit suspicious!

Clayton looks back up at Sheriff Collins and says nothing,
his eyes cut into the Sheriff's soul.

                    SHERIFF COLLINS (CONT'D)
Dear God, you actually believe it.

                    CLAYTON
You'll believe it soon enough too.

Sheriff Collins rubs her temples.

Clayton reaches into his jacket pocket and pulls out an old,
faded photo of a large creature at a long distance away, near
a wooded treeline and hands it to Sheriff Collins. She
studies the picture.

                    SHERIFF COLLINS
I'm sorry Clayton, photos are
easily manipulated these days.
This doesn't prove anything to me.

Clayton ignores her logic.

                    CLAYTON
This is one of the few good pics we
were able to snap of it over the
years. Grand dad kept it secret
after the town's ridicule when he
tried to report it. So the family
gave it plenty of space, and food.
It hibernates in the winter, so we
only worried about it during the
spring & summer. It stayed pretty
content on our land for many years,
but after Dad's sudden death last
year, and the inevitable pipeline
project, I knew I had to come back.

                    SHERIFF COLLINS
I can't believe I'm even listening
to this.

Clayton leans in and looks Sheriff Collins directly in the
eye.

                    CLAYTON
Just give me 3 days. You can stick
to me like glue.
                    (MORE)

                    CLAYTON (CONT'D)
          My team will find it, and prove to
          you that it's real.

                    SHERIFF COLLINS
          Your team?

                    CLAYTON
          I didn't come back alone. They're
          on standby, but can be here in the
          morning. I didn't expect any
          deaths, we thought we could do this
          quietly.

                    SHERIFF COLLINS
          Do what?

Clayton hesitates.

                    CLAYTON
          Relocation.

                    SHERIFF COLLINS
          Relocation?

There is a knock on the two way mirror.

                    SHERIFF COLLINS (CONT'D)
          Excuse me for a minute.

Sheriff Collins leaves the room.

37   EXT. SHERIFF COLLINS HOME - NIGHT   37

Something moves out of the treeline surrounding Sheriff
Collins' home, its face stained with coyote blood. It move
stealthily towards Sadie's window and peers in, Sadie is fast
asleep. Something sniffs around the pane, breathing heavily,
it nudges the window.

Sadie stirs, she sits up and sees Something in the window.
She smiles and crawls out of bed. As she approaches,
Something presses its nose against the window, its breath
pulsating condensation against the glass.

Sadie giggles, she presses her nose against the glass
opposite Something's nose. Something purrs, the quills on
its back ruffle and clatter. It stares into Sadie's eyes
with tenderness. It turns, grabs the dead doe by the hind
legs and casually returns to the treeline.

Sadie watches from her window. Something's eye shine glows
from just inside the trees. Sadie waves, and then retreats
back into bed.

38   INT. POLICE HALLWAY - NIGHT   38

Sheriff Collins exits the interrogation room. Mayor Travis
Stanley is waiting outside.

                         SHERIFF COLLINS
               Mayor?

                         MAYOR
               Sam called me about Clayton.

                         SHERIFF COLLINS
               I'm sorry, I wasn't going to bother
               you about this until tomorrow.

                         MAYOR
               No, it's fine, I'm glad he called.
               So what do you make of his story?

                         SHERIFF COLLINS
               Well, his motor functions don't
               indicate any drug use, so he's
               either suffering from some serious
               PTSD, or he's completely psychotic
               and thinks I'll believe this crazy
               story that his grandfather tried
               telling all those years ago to
               cover up the fact that he's killed
               3 people.

                         MAYOR
               No, I mean about the monster?

                         SHERIFF COLLINS
               Sir?

                         MAYOR
               He sounds pretty convincing.

                         SHERIFF COLLINS
               If it wasn't so absurd, I'd be
               willing to possibly believe it.

                         MAYOR
               Sam says the bodies were a real
               mess. Said it was unlike anything
               he'd ever seen.

                         SHERIFF COLLINS
               Sam's never seen a homicide before,
               he's got no frame of reference.

                         MAYOR
               What about you?

Sheriff Collins looks back at Clayton as she answers.

                    SHERIFF COLLINS
          I don't know yet. I've only dealt
          with a couple of homicides, but I
          have seen lots of animal attacks.
          All of the evidence suggests this
          was too.

Mayor Stanley snatches the photo from Sheriff Collins and
studies it.

                    MAYOR
          Interesting...very interesting.

Sheriff Collins turns her attention back to Mayor Stanley.

                    MAYOR (CONT'D)
          I want you to hold him for 48 hours
          while we gather the evidence from
          the 2 crime scenes and build a case
          to charge him.

                    SHERIFF COLLINS
          There's no evidence to do that.

                    MAYOR
          He was at both crime scenes,
          there's evidence. You may have to
          "creatively" find some, but either
          way, he does not leave that cell!
          Is that understood?

Mayor Stanley walks away. Sheriff Collins physically
disagrees. She enters the interrogation room, Clayton stands
and turns around as Sheriff Collins handcuffs him again.

39   INT. SAM'S DESK - NIGHT   39

Mayor Stanley approaches Sam at his desk.

                    MAYOR
               (to himself)
          I've been waiting more than 40
          years for this moment?

                    SAM
          Waiting for what?

Mayor looks over his shoulder as Sheriff Collins leads
Clayton down the hallway towards the holding cells.

                    MAYOR
               (to Sam)
          You tired of taking orders from a
          woman?

                    SAM
          Every day in every way!

                    MAYOR
          You play your cards right on this
          and you'll end up saving the town,
          and then she won't stand a chance
          against you in the next election.

                    SAM
          You have my attention...keep
          talkin'.

                    MAYOR
          Bring your rifle and meet me at
          Cool Hollow trail tomorrow morning
          at 7:00.

Sam smiles slyly.

                    SAM
          What are we hunting?

                    MAYOR
          A legend...and anything that gets
          in our way.

                    SAM
          Now that's what I'm talkin' about!

                                        FADE OUT.

40   INT. SHERIFF COLLINS OFFICE - SUNRISE   40

Sheriff Collins sits at her desk & types away on her
keyboard, her eyes heavy and hair starting to come out of her
ponytail just a bit. She hits a couple of buttons hard and
turns to her printer as several sheets of paper print out.
She signs the pages in a couple of spots, shuffles the pages
into a thin file folder and deposits it into a file cabinet.

Sheriff Collins slumps back in her chair & stretches. See
glances at the clock on her wall.

CLOCK: 5:47

Sheriff Collins rubs her eyes. She looks at the picture of her family on her desk for a moment, then stands, exits her office, and flips the lights off as she leaves.

41   INT. SHERIFF COLLINS CRUISER - SUNRISE   41

Sheriff Collins drives down a lonely two lane highway, sunglasses on. The sun rising in front of her.

42   EXT. SHERIFF COLLINS HOME - MORNING   42

Sheriff Collins pulls her cruiser into the driveway of her home. She drives to the house and stops the car in front of the garage, kills the engine, and exits.

The woods are still in the distance.

43   INT. SHERIFF COLLINS HOME - MORNING   43

Sheriff Collins enters the front door, being as quiet as possible. She sets the keys on the table, tiptoes down the hall, and enters a room.

                                                  CUT TO:

44   INT. SHERIFF COLLINS BEDROOM - MORNING   44

Sheriff Collins removes her gun belt, sets it on the dresser, extracts her gun and locks it away in a wall-mounted gun case.

Sheriff Collins removes her uniform down to a sports bra & pulls on a pair of shorts before climbing into bed next to Jake.

Jake stirs, Sheriff Collins watches him sleep as her eyes grow heavy and eventually shut.

                                              FADE TO BLACK.

45   EXT. COOL HOLLOW TRAIL - MORNING   45

Sam stands next to his pick-up truck, dressed in overalls with a high powered rifle as Mayor Stanley pulls up and parks behind it. Mayor Stanley exits his vehicle, dressed in camouflage and toting a rifle of his own.

                        SAM
              Morning, Mayor.

Mayor Stanley hands Sam his rifle, reaches into his pocket and hands Sam a handful of ammunition.

                    MAYOR
          Load this, will ya?

Sam sets his rifle down against his truck.

                    SAM
          You don't know how to load your
          rifle?

Mayor Stanley stares Sam down.

                    MAYOR
          Just do it!

Sam loads the rifle for Mayor Stanley and hands it back.

                    MAYOR (CONT'D)
          Now, are you ready to make history?

                    SAM
          If you mean blowing a hole through
          the head of some dumb animal as
          making history, then you can call
          me George Washington.

                    MAYOR
          Yeah, that's great, but just so
          we're clear on how this is going to
          go down, you're job is to find it,
          I'll be taking the shot.

Sam shakes the leftover loose ammunition in his hand.

                    SAM
          Is that so?

Mayor Stanley faces off with Sam.

                    MAYOR
          Yeah, that's so. Now, I brought
          you along for this ride, but I'm in
          charge here. Understood?

Sam hands the ammunition back to Mayor Stanley as they both keep their eyes locked on each other.

                    SAM
          Understood.

Mayor Stanley trudges onto the trail and heads into the forest.

                    SAM (CONT'D)
                 (under his breath)
            Need someone to show you how to
            pull the trigger too?

Sam follows after Mayor Stanley.

                                              CUT TO:

46   INT. SHERIFF COLLINS BEDROOM - AFTERNOON   46

Sheriff Collins wakes, Jake is gone from the bed. She sits
up, and can hear voices from somewhere in the house. She
exits bed, removes the shorts, and puts on a pair of jeans
with holes in the knees.

She hears the door open and close.

47   EXT. SHERIFF COLLINS HOME - AFTERNOON   47

Sheriff Collins exits the house from the front door. Jake &
Sadie are sitting on a blanket in the front yard, having a
picnic. They look up to see Sheriff Collins squinting at
them from the sunlight.

                        SADIE
            MOMMY!

Sadie jumps up and runs to her mother, giving her a big hug.
Sheriff Collins hugs Sadie, and kisses the top of her head.

                    SHERIFF COLLINS
            How are you sweetheart?

                        SADIE
            Good! I missed you.

                    SHERIFF COLLINS
            I missed you too, baby.

Jake stands and approaches.

                    SHERIFF COLLINS (CONT'D)
            I'll be over for the picnic in a
            minute, can you set my place for
            me?

                        SADIE
            Uh-huh.

Sadie runs off to the blanket. Jake embraces Sheriff
Collins, they kiss.

                    JAKE
          Good morning, Sleepy Head.

                    SHERIFF COLLINS
          Is it morning still?

                    JAKE
          It is to you. Long night?

                    SHERIFF COLLINS
          Triple terminal night, guess you
          could say I'm dead tired.

Jake looks pained, Sheriff Collins smiles.

                    JAKE
          Damn, anyone we knew?

                    SHERIFF COLLINS
          No, some young guy from Mount
          Pleasant and two hunters from out
          of town.

                    JAKE
          What happened?

                    SHERIFF COLLINS
          Not sure...

                                                  CUT TO:

Sadie is retrieving a cookie for her mother when a slight
breeze comes up and blows Sheriff Collins' plate from the
blanket, tumbling across the yard. Sadie stands and gives
chase.

The plate stops about ten yards from the tree line. Sadie
catches up to it and picks up the plate. A low grunt is
heard from within the trees. She stands facing the forest.

                                                  CUT TO:

                    SHERIFF COLLINS (CONT'D)
          ...but we were leaning toward an
          animal attack until Clayton Sawyer
          showed up at both locations.

                    JAKE
          Clayton's back?

                    SHERIFF COLLINS
          Yeah, but he's not the same as he
          used to be.

48   EXT. COOL HOLLOW TRAIL - DAY   48

Sam trots briskly to catch up to Mayor Stanley.

                    SAM
          You ever fired a rifle before?

                    MAYOR
          Nope, but it can't be too hard.
          This thing is supposed to be huge.
          Aim & pull the trigger.

Sam shakes his head side to side, let's out a chuckle.

                    SAM
          Hold up, just a second.

Mayor Stanley stops and faces Sam abruptly. Sam leans
forward and flips the safety on of Mayor Stanley's rifle.

                    SAM (CONT'D)
          If I'm leading, your safety stays
          ON until the target is in sight,
          and I'm out of the way.

Mayor Stanley scoffs, flips the safety off points at a large
oak tree. Mayor Stanley pulls his rifle up to his chest. Lays
the stock under his armpit, and brings his head down to the
scope before lifting the barrel up at the tree. Sam rolls
his eyes. Mayor Stanley pulls the trigger, his arms flail
wildly from the recoil. The bullet misses the target
completely.

49   EXT. SHERIFF COLLINS HOME - DAY   49

A gunshot rings out from deep into the forest. Something
snaps its head toward the sound, its quills lay down, its
ears fold back as it gives a deep guttural growl toward the
noise.

Jake & Sheriff Collins turn to the blanket, Sadie is not
there. Jake turns again searching for her.

Sadie takes steps closer to the trees.

                    JAKE
          SADIE! Stay close please!

50   EXT. COOL HOLLOW TRAIL - DAY   50

Sam steps forward, casually clapping his hands.

> SAM
> Well, aren't you a regular Lucas
> McCain?

Mayor Stanley chambers another round, pulls the rifle up
again.

> SAM (CONT'D)
> Hold tight.

Sam helps position the gun properly as he explains.

> SAM (CONT'D)
> Stock against your shoulder, bring
> the barrel up to your line of
> sight, lean forward slightly.

Mayor Stanley shoots at the tree again, bullet grazes the
side as bark flies off.

> SAM (CONT'D)
> Better. Next time breathe in as you
> aim, and pull the trigger at the
> end of your exhale.

51   EXT. SHERIFF COLLINS HOME - DAY   51

Sheriff Collins raises her hand over her eyes, shielding the
sun, to get a better look at Sadie's location. Sadie turns
and waves at Sheriff Collins, she smiles and turns her
attention back to Jake.

> JAKE
> What do you mean he's not the same?

                                                  CUT TO:

Something grunts its displeasure and turns back to Sadie.

Sadie holds the cookie up toward the trees. She smiles
kindly as a tall set of quills and a thick back rise up.

Something bursts from the woods, scoops up Sadie in its arms,
and retreats with lightning speed.

                                                  CUT TO:

The commotion draws Sheriff Collins & Jake's attention. The
tree tops sway moving away from the treeline, and Sadie is
not there.

> SHERIFF COLLINS
> SADIE?

Sheriff Collins & Jake run toward the trees. The sound of snapping branches and rustling can be heard in the distance within the forest.

                    JAKE
          SADIE!

Sheriff Collins steps inside the tree line. a few feet in she finds the dead doe, most of the body has been consumed. Next to it, imprinted in the forest floor, are the same knuckle prints that she's seen at both crime scenes. Sheriff Collins stares deep into the woods for any sign.

                    SHERIFF COLLINS
          Oh dear lord...

Jake enters the woods next to Sheriff Collins.

                    SHERIFF COLLINS (CONT'D)
          It took her.

                    JAKE
          What took her?

Sheriff Collins looks frantically at Jake.

                    SHERIFF COLLINS
          Clayton's monster.

Sheriff Collins turns and runs out of the woods towards her car. Jake watches for a moment and then turns and runs into the woods after Sadie.

52   EXT. COOL HOLLOW TRAIL - DAY   52

Sam leads Mayor Stanley on the trail and diverts through the timber a few yards until he's reached the wooded campsite of the hunters. Yellow crime scene tape has been strung around the area, Mayor Stanley ducks underneath it and enters, Sam follows.

                    MAYOR
          Look for prints.

Sam breaks from Mayor Stanley and goes immediately to the tree where Hunter 1's body was found. Knuckle prints distinctly can be seen entering the campsite up to the tree, and then they stop. Sam scans up the tree, bark has been torn away.

                    SAM
          It can climb.

Sam looks at a couple surrounding trees, they seem
undisturbed, and turns his attention back to the ground, but
outward from the tree farther. Sam finds the print from
where the monster landed.

                    SAM (CONT'D)
          Got it!

Sam follows the commotion of the tracks, getting misled a
couple times before finding the location again. It leads him
to the hang line of the coyotes. Mayor Stanley stands next
to Sam.

                    MAYOR
          What is it?

                    SAM
          It took their kill.

                    MAYOR
          Which way did it go?

Sam points to his right.

                    SAM
          That way.

                    MAYOR
          Then what the hell are you waiting
          for?

Sam eyes the Mayor and walks out of the campsite and into the
forest.

53   INT. JAIL - DAY   53

Sheriff Collins bursts through the doors of the holding cell
area, carrying a pair of military boots. She walks to cell
#3 and unlocks it.

54   INT. CELL 3 - DAY   54

Clayton sits up in bed as Sheriff Collins opens the cell
door. She tosses his boots into the middle of floor.

                    SHERIFF COLLINS
          Put 'em on, let's go!

                    CLAYTON
          Where to?

> SHERIFF COLLINS
> It took my daughter.

Sheriff Collins disappears out of the cell door, Clayton jumps up from bed, grabs his boots and follows.

55   INT. JAIL - DAY   55

Clayton catches up to Sheriff Collins, she hands him a cell phone.

> CLAYTON
> How long ago?

> SHERIFF COLLINS
> 30 minutes. Call your team, have
> 'em meet at my house. We'll pick
> up the trail from there.

Clayton swipes the screen on, taps it, and holds it to his ear.

> CLAYTON
> (into the phone)
> Hey, you're up.

CUT TO:

56   EXT. FOREST - DAY   56

Something storms through the forest, finds a clearing, and stops to survey the area. Something puts Sadie down next to some thick brush & heavy ferns, she is smudged with dirt, and some scratches from the trip through the forest.

Something withdraws a few feet away and watches Sadie.

Sadie rights herself from the ground and wipes the hair from her face. She looks at Something. She smiles, something looks away. Sadie stands and slowly walks toward Something.

> SADIE
> Are you hungry?

Something turns back to her and watches.

> SADIE (CONT'D)
> It's peanut butter.

Sadie holds the cookie up to Something, it sniffs the air toward Sadie, its breath heavy & loud.

                    SADIE (CONT'D)
          You can eat it. I have more at my
          picnic.

Something leans down and with extremely gentle grace, takes
the cookie from Sadie and slowly puts it in its mouth. Sadie
smiles.

                    SADIE (CONT'D)
          I'm Sadie.

A distant & vague voice in the forest draws Something's
attention. It quickly sniffs the air, its eyes narrow and
its mouth tightens as it rumbles a growl from deep within
it's chest. The voices get closer. Something pushes Sadie
behind it and they back up slowly, watching the forest in
front of it with distrust the entire time and disappearing
into the heavy brush & ferns. Its quills rising above the
brush.

On the other side of the clearing, Mayor Stanley & Sam enter
from the forest. Sam stalks the ground.

Something's quills slowly lay down and disappear into the
brush.

Sam stops about half way across the clearing, and takes a
deep breath while Mayor Stanley almost runs into him.

                    MAYOR
          What is it?

                    SAM
          You smell that?

Mayor smells the air.

                    MAYOR
          Smell what?

                    SAM
          That musty animal smell.

                    MAYOR
          The whole damn forest smells like
          an animal toilet!

Sam grips his rifle in both hands and waits. Noises come
from deep in the forest in front of Sam & the mayor.

Something starts to tense in the brush.

                    SAM
               (whispering over his
                shoulder)
          It's close.

Sam motions for Mayor Stanley to take cover behind a tree to
his right, and he does. Mayor Stanley points his rifle
toward the forest noise, as it gets louder.

Sam hunkers down behind a log, peering through his sight, gun
aimed ready.

Jake suddenly bursts through the trees and into the clearing,
Mayor Stanley fires one round that misses Jake by a long
shot. Jake ducks down quickly, and puts his hands out in
front of him.

                    SAM (CONT'D)
          Cease fire!

                    MAYOR
          Son-of-a-bitch!

Mayor comes out from behind the tree.

                    MAYOR (CONT'D)
          Jake, what the hell are you doing
          out here?

                    JAKE
          Sadie is missing.

Sam ups from the log and joins the Mayor & Jake.

                    MAYOR
          What do you mean missing?

                    JAKE
          Something took her. Something big.
          Casey said it was Clayton's
          monster.

                    MAYOR
          Where is your wife?

                    JAKE
          I think she went to get help.

Mayor turns to Sam.

                    MAYOR
          You get a call?

Sam leans in to the Mayor and whispers.

                    SAM
          Clayton.

Mayor Stanley is visibly agitated. He turns back to Jake.

                    MAYOR
          Jake, you need to go back home and
          wait for your wife. Sam & I will
          find Sadie.

                    JAKE
          I'm not leaving these woods until I
          find my little girl.

Sam smells the air again. He looks down on the ground. He
sees knuckle prints, and next to them the grid prints of a
child's shoes. Sam follows the tracks into the heavy brush.

                    MAYOR
          Jake, this is an order, not an
          option. Go home. NOW!

Sam interrupts.

                    SAM
          You two need to shut the fuck up!

Jake & Mayor Stanley turn toward Sam. The quills from
Something slowly rise up from the brush, and then collapse
down again halfway.

                    SAM (CONT'D)
          It's here with us.

Sam steps forward a few steps toward the quills. A loud
guttural purring comes from within the brush. Mayor Stanley
raises his rifle too. The quills spring up quickly, a few fly
off of Something's back like bullets and lodge into a tree
branch about 30 feet up. Sam follows the quills with his
rifle and shoots at them, the mayor does the same.

Something leaps out of the brush and lands between Sam and
Mayor Stanley. It roars tremendously loud, Mayor Stanley
cowers as Jake falls down. Sam spins with his rifle aimed,
Something swings its arm and knocks Sam across the rest of
the clearing and into the brush.

Something turns its attention back to Mayor Stanley, as Sadie
emerges from the brush and trots up to the side of Something.
Mayor Stanley raises his rifle, Jake jumps up and reacts
quickly.

                    JAKE
          NO!

Jake knocks the gun off its mark, Something grabs Sadie and pulls her out of the way of the bullet as it flies off into the brush, hitting Sam in the leg. Sam screams.

                    MAYOR
          God damn it, Jake!

The Mayor turns the rifle around and cracks Jake in the back of the head. Jake drops unconscious. Sadie reacts.

                    SADIE
               Daddy!

Something roars and charges at Mayor Stanley, covering the ground between them in seconds.

                    MAYOR
               Oh shit!

Mayor Stanley backpedals and dives behind his tree just as Something swipes at him with its open hand. Something misses the mayor and tears a huge chunk from the side of the tree. The wood debris showers over Mayor Stanley as he rolls down a banking and disappears into some brush.

Something turns quickly and retreats to Sadie, again scooping her up and charging quickly out of the clearing, disappearing into the forest.

                                        CUT TO:

57   EXT. SHERIFF COLLINS HOME - AFTERNOON   57

Clayton stands over the hood of the Sheriff's cruiser, a map of Jefferson County is spread over it. Clayton plots points on the map, as Sheriff Collins exits the house strapping her gun belt around her waist. She opens the cruiser door, pulls out her shotgun, and tosses it to Clayton.

                    SHERIFF COLLINS
          How soon before your team arrives?

A large YUKON pulls off the road and into the driveway.

                    CLAYTON
          Look no further.

The Yukon pulls up the Clayton & Sheriff Collins, it stops abruptly. The driver door opens up and an extremely large & muscular African American man, VAUGHN TENNYSON (40s) exits and heads immediately to the back of the Yukon, pops the door and begins to unload equipment.

The other doors open, from the front passengers door is
SEWERYNA GRABOWSKI (40s), heavily tattooed arms, hair pulled
back, huge crescent moon scar running from her forehead on
the right side of her face, ending under the left side of her
chin.

STASHUE "SWAT" MIRNOWSKI, (30s) emerges from the rear
passenger seat. Shaved head, expressionless, cold,
calculating.

KORI GRABOWSKI (teens) leaves the rear drivers door.

Seweryna approaches Clayton & Sheriff Collins as the others
help Vaughn.

                    CLAYTON (CONT'D)
          Sheriff Collins, this is Seweryna
          Grabowski. She'll take over from
          here.

                    SHERIFF COLLINS
          Thank you for coming.

Sheriff Collins holds out her hand to shake. Seweryna bellows
to her team.

                    SEWERYNA
          Pospiesz sie!

Seweryna ignores the outstretched hand and speaks eye to eye
with Sheriff Collins as she approaches Clayton at the hood of
the cruiser.

                    SEWERYNA (CONT'D)
          You'll have to excuse my informal
          impression, Sheriff. It's my
          understanding that we were a bit
          late in arriving before any
          problems started and now they've
          escalated to a point that a very
          young, very needy girl is involved.

                    CLAYTON
          It's the Sheriff's daughter.

                    SHERIFF COLLINS
          Sadie.

The rest of the team is busy behind. Seweryna motions to
them.

> SEWERYNA
> This will be our base camp. They
> will have it operational in 15
> minutes. If either of you are not
> ready by that time then you're on
> your own.

> CLAYTON
> We're ready now.

> SEWERYNA
> We've studied the footage you gave
> us, and we are dealing with a very
> large, very bright, self aware,
> sentient creature. It's shy, and
> does not like to be detected, and
> therefore is nocturnal by choice.
> Currently it is seeking a place to
> retire until the evening, and once
> it's found someplace it considers
> safe, that gives us one very small
> chance of finding your offspring...

Sheriff Collins interrupts.

> SHERIFF COLLINS
> Sadie!

> SEWERYNA
> ...before nightfall, and then our
> job becomes progressively harder.

Vaughn approaches them, hands Clayton & Seweryna small
devices, both tilting their heads to the side to put the
device into their ear. Vaughn stands next to Sheriff
Collins.

> VAUGHN
> It's a communication device, fits
> in your ear canal. You'll be able
> to hear and respond to Kori here at
> base camp.

Sheriff Collins takes the earpiece, tilts her head, and
maneuvers it in place. Vaughn retreats back to helping the
others.

Seweryna turns from Sheriff Collins and studies the map with
Clayton.

> SEWERYNA
> Hot spots?

Clayton points to circles plotted on the map.

                    CLAYTON
          This is my old land, and the
          current site of the pumping
          station. This is the site of the
          hunters' camp.

Seweryna points to a plot.

                    SEWERYNA
          This must be home base?

                    CLAYTON
          Yes.

                    SEWERYNA
          So then what is this?

Seweryna points to a plot quite a ways away from the others.
Sheriff Collins leans in to see.

                    CLAYTON
          That's where it hibernates in the
          winter.

                    SHERIFF COLLINS
          The Devil's Cookie Jar?

                    CLAYTON
          Yes.

Seweryna leaves the cruiser and meets Swat in front of the
Yukon.

                    SEWERYNA
          That's our focus then!

Sheriff Collins interrupts again.

                    SHERIFF COLLINS
          That's not the way it headed
          earlier!

Swat walks past the Yukon and grabs the map off the hood.

                    SWAT
          But that's where it's going.

                    SHERIFF COLLINS
          How do you figure?

Seweryna secures her vest as Swat hands the map to Kori.

                    SEWERYNA
          Tell me Sheriff, when you respond
          to a domestic violence call, where
          is the first place a victim will go
          to get away from their abuser?

                    SHERIFF COLLINS
          Usually to their parents, if they
          live close by.

                    SEWERYNA
          The place they feel safest! Trust
          me, it's not there now, but that's
          where it's headed.

Seweryna and the rest of her team disappear to the back of
the Yukon. Clayton starts to follow them and is stopped by
Sheriff Collins.

                    SHERIFF COLLINS
          That's 90 degrees in the opposite
          way this thing headed with my
          daughter, and my husband is out
          there after her.

                    CLAYTON
          I know, but these guys are top tier
          hunters. They know how animals
          think, they are known for being one
          step ahead of them. They are your
          best chance to get your daughter
          back.

                    SHERIFF COLLINS
          You are my best chance to get my
          daughter back!

Clayton is torn.

                    CLAYTON
          You want to follow the tracks,
          don't you?

                    SHERIFF COLLINS
          Yes!

Clayton looks at the team, they are finishing their
preparations.

                    CLAYTON
          OK, I'll come with you, but if we
          hit a dead end, you agree that
          we'll meet back up with the team.

                    SHERIFF COLLINS
               Fine, agreed!

Clayton leaves and talks to the team behind the Yukon.
Seweryna, Swat, & Vaughn all head back toward Sheriff
Collins, all are heavily armed. Seweryna speaks as she walks
past Sheriff Collins.

                    SEWERYNA
               It's displaced, in a foreign land
               right now, but it will find its way
               home...

Seweryna looks Sheriff Collins directly in the eye as she
passes her.

                    SEWERYNA (CONT'D)
               ...and we'll be waiting for it.

The team keeps walking and disappears into the woods.
Clayton stands next to Sheriff Collins. Kori meets up with
them.

                    KORI
               I've put you both on channel two.
               I can watch both teams from here on
               the infrared satellite tracking.

                    CLAYTON
               Thanks, Kori.

                    KORI
               Don't mention it.

                    CLAYTON
                    (to Sheriff Collins)
               Are you ready?

Sheriff Collins nods and they both head in the direction that
Sadie was last seen and disappear into the forest. Kori
settles in at her chair in front of multiple laptops and
types coordinates from the map into one.

58   EXT. FOREST - DAY   58

Mayor Stanley crawls back up the embankment slowly. He scans
the area, all is calm until Sam stumbles out of the brush,
tying a strap around his leg just above his blood stained
pants. Mayor Stanley joins him in the clearing.

                    SAM
               You shot me, you asshole.

> MAYOR
>> I exhaled!

Sam is not pleased by the mayor's response.

> SAM
>> You don't shoot anything from now
>> on unless it's 5 feet away.
>> Understand?

Mayor Stanley ignores him and removes Sam's handcuffs from
his belt. Mayor Stanley squats down and cuffs Jake's hands
behind his back. He then starts to slap Jake lightly on the
face repeatedly.

> MAYOR
>> Wake up!

Jake stirs, his eyes open in slits. Mayor stands back up.

> MAYOR (CONT'D)
>> Let's go.

Mayor kicks Jake's legs.

> MAYOR (CONT'D)
>> Get up.

> JAKE
>> Where's Sadie?

> SAM
>> He said get up!

> JAKE
>> My head hurts.

Jake tries to move his arms but can't.

> JAKE (CONT'D)
>> What's going on?

> MAYOR
>> You're being detained, for
>> obstruction!

> JAKE
>> Obstruction?

> SAM
>> That's right! Now, get up!

Mayor Stanley kicks Jake's leg again. Jake struggles to get
to his feet, he's wobbly.

                    MAYOR
                  (to Sam)
             Which way?

                    SAM
             Saw it leave with the kid through
             there.

Sam points the direction Something took.

                    MAYOR
             Let's get moving!

Sam hobbles toward the forest. Mayor Stanley points the gun
at Jake, who follows. All three men disappear into the
woods.

59   EXT. FOREST - AFTERNOON   59

Something charges through the trees. It stops and looks
around, sets Sadie down. Something yawns and slumps against
a large tree, which creaks & moans from the weight.

Sadie looks around, she spies a wildflower growing. She
smiles brightly, plucks it, and inhales it's petals deeply.
Sadie calmly approaches Something and offers the wildflower
with an outstretched hand.

                    SADIE
             This is for you.

Something looks down at Sadie. It reaches for the flower,
and gently takes it from her.

                    SADIE (CONT'D)
             It's pretty. It smells pretty.
             You have to smell it.

Sadie taps her nose and inhales deeply. Something looks at
the flower and lifts it to its nose, inhales deeply, and
sneezes abruptly. Sadie falls down. She giggles. Something
drops the flower, Sadie picks it up and tries to put it in
her own hair but can't. Something reaches down, takes the
flower from her again, and gently puts it securely into
Sadie's hair.

                    SADIE (CONT'D)
             Thank you.

Distant voices of Sam & Mayor Stanley pull Something's
immediate attention. It scoops up Sadie and swiftly climbs
the tree without incident.

Debris falls from the tops of the trees leading away from the
location Something & Sadie just were. Eighty feet away
Something, carrying Sadie, scurries down another large tree,
and sinks into the brush on the forest floor, completely
obscuring itself & Sadie from view.

Voices grow louder, and eventually Sam stumbles along the
path of Something. Trudging behind Sam comes Jake followed
by Mayor Stanley. Sam stops at the tree.

                    SAM
          Hold up.

Something watches the men from its hidden location. Sadie
huddles next to it, silent. Something snarls quietly.

                    MAYOR
          What now?

Sam observes the direct area, and then scans up the tree.

                    SAM
          It's in the trees.

                    MAYOR
          What?

                    JAKE
          Is Sadie still with it?

                    SAM
          It knows it's being followed, so it
          took a route that we can't follow.

                    MAYOR
          How the hell can it know that?

                    JAKE
          What's happened to Sadie?

Mayor Stanley pushes Jake to the ground.

                    MAYOR
          Shut the hell up!

Sadie & Something continue to watch the men.

                    SAM
          Well, it appears to be smarter than
          you think it is!

                    MAYOR
          So which way is it going?

Sam opens an electronic GPS device and plots coordinates into it. Mayor Stanley watches the screen. The GPS device maps the path and gives a probable coordinate of destination.

> SAM
> According to this, the current path
> it's taking is random, almost like
> it's lost and looking for something
> familiar. In the general
> direction, there's a 62% chance
> that it's destination is here.

Sam hits a button on the GPS, it scans ahead on the map 5.4 miles from their current location.

Jake removes his cell phone from his back pocket, slips his hands to the front of his body. And hits his voice recorder, and shuffles it under his body.

> MAYOR
> Where is that?

> SAM
> It's heading to the Devil's Cookie
> Jar.

> MAYOR
> The gully & cave systems?

Sam nods. Jake tries to stand.

> JAKE
> Tell me Sadie is still...

Sam reacts, pulling his HANDGUN and sticking the barrel directly in the center of Jake's forehead.

> SAM
> He said to shut up! You best shut
> the fuck up!

Sadie buries her head into Something's arm, unable to watch.

Jake freezes. Sam leans in closer to Jake.

> SAM (CONT'D)
> You & your daughter are not
> supposed to be here! Don't think
> for one second that I won't take
> you out of this equation.
> (MORE)

                    SAM (CONT'D)
          Hell, if the wildlife doesn't get
          you, I'll be the one who'll head
          the investigation, and what really
          happened will never come to light
          anyway. So just keep testing me!

Sam pulls the gun away slowly, as Jake relaxes and stays
silent.

                    MAYOR
          Enough. Wait until we kill it, and
          then you can take out Old Jake here
          too.

Mayor Stanley smiles sinisterly at Jake.

Sam turns his attention back to the GPS.

                    SAM
          It's this way.

                    MAYOR
          Then let's get moving. By the time
          we get there, it'll be dark.

Mayor pulls Jake to his feet and they continue on through the
forest. Jake's cell phone stays on the ground, unnoticed.

Something watches them as they leave the area. Sadie curls
up closer, and something curls in tighter. They both shut
their eyes.

60   EXT. FOREST - AFTERNOON   60

Vaughn leads Seweryna's team through the forest, all walking
with purpose.

                    KORI
               (through earpiece)
          About 2.1 miles dead ahead. Stay on
          course.

                    VAUGHN
          Looks like we'll have about an hour
          of daylight once we get there.

                    SWAT
          Enough time to survey the area and
          arrange a triangular attack
          position.

                    SEWERYNA
          Once at the site, I want Vaughn on
          weapons & FLIR, Swat will arrange
          for team locations. I'll handle
          the bait.

The team moves swiftly through the forest and disappears.

61   EXT. FOREST CLEARING - AFTERNOON   61

Sheriff Collins & Clayton survey the area, it's in disarray.
Clayton squats to look at Sam's blood on the ground.

                    CLAYTON
          There's blood here.

The statement draws Sheriff Collins' attention.

                    SHERIFF COLLINS
          Who's is it? Sadie's?

Clayton & Sheriff Collins follow the blood trail.

                    CLAYTON
          I don't think so. It trails away
          from here. Someone who's wearing
          boots.

Sheriff Collins is relieved, and spies tiny footprints.

                    SHERIFF COLLINS
          She was here though.

                    CLAYTON
          Yep.

                    SHERIFF COLLINS
          But this isn't Jake's blood either.
          He was wearing tennis shoes.

Clayton & Sheriff Collins follow the trail across the
clearing.

                    CLAYTON
          So who else is with them?

Sheriff Collins looks closer at the bleeding boot print, then
looks back at her own prints. They are the exact same, only
smaller.

                    SHERIFF COLLINS
          Oh thank God. It's Sam!

Clayton steps away and stares up.

                    CLAYTON
          Hey, check this out.

Clayton points up at the quills stuck into the tree branch.
Sheriff Collins joins him.

                    SHERIFF COLLINS
          Hey, I saw one of those in the
          cornfield yesterday. Are those...

                    CLAYTON
               (interrupts)
          Quills? Yes. It uses them as a
          distraction, to make itself seem
          bigger during a confrontation.

                    SHERIFF COLLINS
          It shoots its quills?

                    CLAYTON
          Not really "shoots," more like
          raising them so quickly that they
          dislodge.

                    SHERIFF COLLINS
          That makes perfect sense of the
          coyote tracks in the cornfield.
          They were after its kill. It lost
          one trying to scare them off.

Clayton points into the woods, he & Sheriff Collins walk in
that direction, Clayton puts his fingers up to his earpiece.

                    CLAYTON
          Kori, we're heading west. Anything
          in that same direction?

                    KORI
               (through earpiece)
          Not that I can see. Just takes you
          deeper into the woods.

                    SHERIFF COLLINS
          Where is the other team from us?

                    KORI
               (through earpiece)
          North west about 7 miles.

                    CLAYTON
              (to Sheriff Collins)
         Well, they're kinda in the same
         area.

Sheriff Collins examines the void missing from the tree, deep
grooves where Something's fingers ripped through the wood are
visible. Sheriff Collins runs her hand over them.

                    SHERIFF COLLINS
         What on earth could do this?

                    CLAYTON
         Kori, can you scan the radar
         between us & Seweryna?

                    KORI
              (through earpiece)
         One second...

                                                  CUT TO:

62   EXT. SHERIFF COLLINS HOME - AFTERNOON   62

Kori types away on a laptop. A United States map emerges on
screen, and the screen begins to zoom into Iowa continuing to
a grid of 20 square miles. 3 different blips are shown in
the grid.

                    KORI
         Looks like there is an anomaly
         north of you by a couple of miles.
         It doesn't appear to be moving.
              (beat)
         Wait a second, it is moving, but
         very slowly.

                                                  CUT TO:

63   EXT. FOREST CLEARING - AFTERNOON   63

Clayton pulls Sheriff Collins away from the tree.

                    CLAYTON
         We can catch up.

Sheriff Collins and Clayton quicken their pace and leave the
clearing, following the same trail.

64   EXT. FOREST TRAIL - AFTERNOON   64

Sheriff Collins trails Clayton as he moves through the forest
with purpose.

                    SHERIFF COLLINS
               Did you see that tree?

                    CLAYTON
               Yes, I saw the tree.

                    SHERIFF COLLINS
               So what did that?

                    CLAYTON
               You know what. I told you back at
               the station.

Sheriff Collins speeds up to catch Clayton. She grabs him by
the shoulder and spins him around to face her.

                    SHERIFF COLLINS
               Listen, I'm still the Sheriff of
               this county, so you better start
               telling me what the hell we're
               dealing with here, because my
               family is neck deep in some serious
               shit and you seem to be the only
               one who has a clue how to handle
               this situation.

Clayton rubs his head from the stress of the entire
situation. He backs up and leans against a tree.

                    CLAYTON
               I'm not entirely sure where to
               start. It just showed up on my
               grandfather's farm back in the
               70's.

Sheriff Collins interrupts.

                    SHERIFF COLLINS
               You can walk & talk at the same
               time. Keep moving.

Clayton sets off again through the woods, but has slowed a
bit.

                    CLAYTON
               We never found out what it was. It
               kept coming back to the farm almost
               nighty to raid his chicken coop.
                         (MORE)

                    CLAYTON (CONT'D)
          Grand dad lost his entire stock
          that summer. He sat up in the hay
          loft one night waiting to put a
          bullet between it's eyes, but it
          knew Grand dad was there and stared
          him down from the empty coop, said
          that moment changed him as a man.
          Said he could see the intelligence
          & sincerity behind its eyes, and
          considered himself compared to the
          monster. That's when he realized
          that they were both just trying to
          survive in a world that meant to be
          shared by all creatures. It's what
          pushed him to stop farming animals
          and go to straight organic crops.

                    SHERIFF COLLINS
          I remember when he first started
          talking about what he had seen.

                    CLAYTON
          Nobody believed him. Dad said he
          wanted so badly to prove to
          everyone that the monster was real.
          He was determined to kill it to
          prove everyone wrong. Imagine
          Dad's surprise when Grand dad
          stopped allowing hunters on his
          property. That gave it plenty of
          deer to hunt on its own.

                    SHERIFF COLLINS
          So he took it upon himself to keep
          it safe?

                    CLAYTON
          Yeah, and it made our land its
          home. It stuck around all spring &
          summer, year after year. It would
          disappear during the winter, but
          it'd always be back.

                    SHERIFF COLLINS
          So your whole family knew about
          this thing?

                    CLAYTON
          Us & Travis.

                    SHERIFF COLLINS
          Travis? As in Mayor Stanley?

                    CLAYTON
          Yes ma'am, he was Grand dad's
          farmhand.

                    SHERIFF COLLINS
          So why did it take Sadie?

Clayton stops and looks back at Sheriff Collins.

                    CLAYTON
          Once I remember Dad talking about
          how he'd seen it kill a deer, and
          then a few minutes later the fawn
          came stumbling out of the forest
          looking for its mother. Dad said
          the monster carried the dead deer
          up to the ridge of a hill. The
          fawn followed, and when it spotted
          the rest of the herd on the other
          side, the fawn ran to them and
          escaped into the woods. It seems
          to understand sincerity, and
          helplessness. I think it's simply
          trying to protect a vulnerable life
          from what it perceives as an
          invasion into its new territory.

                    SHERIFF COLLINS
          Do you really think it's wise to
          relocate it? It's killed three
          people so far.

                    CLAYTON
          There are levels of personal
          appreciation that people go
          through, most don't reach it until
          much later in life. In the war, I
          saw the worst that humanity has to
          offer, and it really pushes you to
          look at life differently. Not just
          human life, but all life.
          We need all life if we are to
          survive as a species, yet we can't
          even keep from destroying our own
          planet year after year. If one
          species is eradicated from
          existence, all others will suffer
          the consequences to some degree.

                    SHERIFF COLLINS
          So saving one life saves all lives?

                    CLAYTON
          Exactly.

Sheriff Collins & Clayton continue walking through the forest trail.

65   EXT. FOREST - DUSK   65

Something nuzzles with Sadie inside the brush cover. Voices of Sheriff Collins & Clayton can be heard in the distance. Something wakes and listens. It growls its displeasure, pulls Sadie up, and retreats from its hiding spot.

Something charges through the woods up and over an embankment. In the distance is a run down trailer in the middle of a field. Something hears the voices getting closer and heads in the direction of the trailer.

66   EXT. DEVIL'S COOKIE JAR - DUSK   66

Seweryna looks over the edge of the natural gully which descends down about seventy feet below. The rest of the team follows up behind her.

                    SEWERYNA
          Jackpot.

Swat surveys the area.

                    SWAT
          That looks like a perfect sniper
          position.

Swat points to a rocky outcropping across the other side of gully, while Vaughn starts to ready rappelling rope.

                    SEWERYNA
          It's a large area. Lot of
          variables. We need to get down
          there to decide.

                    VAUGHN
          I'm surprised it doesn't just live
          here. It's big enough, isolated,
          with a water supply.

Vaughn points out a small stream running along the wall at the bottom of the gully.

                    SEWERYNA
          It can't, no food supply.

Swat heads off along the ridge. Vaughn starts to tie off the rappel line to a tree, then throws the rest of the slack over the edge.

                    VAUGHN
          After you.

Seweryna pulls the gloves tight on her hands, grabs the rope,
slides instantly down, and disappears over the ledge.

67   EXT. FOREST - DUSK   67

Mayor Stanley follows Jake at gunpoint behind Sam as they
trek through the forest. Sam stops and looks around.

                    MAYOR
          This is the third time you've
          stopped in the last 10 minutes.

                    SAM
          Yeah, you want to lead?

                    MAYOR
          What's the problem?

                    SAM
          What? You mean other than the fact
          that you shot me?

                    MAYOR
          You want me to check my pockets for
          some Bactine?

                    SAM
          Fuck you!

Mayor Stanley leans over Jake's shoulder, close to Sam.

                    MAYOR
          Move it!

                                              CUT TO:

68   EXT. TRAILER - DUSK   68

A young lady, LISA EVERS (30s), dressed in filthy attire and
no shoes, mills about the outside of the old abandoned
trailer. The materials of a meth lab are strung about the
yard, and inside the open door of the trailer. Lisa's
movements are excessive, and constant, clearly not of a
normal person.

Lisa stumbles through the overgrown property, mumbling &
physically unable to control herself as Sadie casually walks
out of the cornfield twenty yards away.

                    LISA
          Where are you? Why are you here?
          Where are you? You can't be here,
          you'll ruin it. Go away!

Sadie is uncertain of Lisa's fast talking and sporadic
physical movements. She looks back at the corn. Lisa starts
walking quickly and unevenly toward Sadie.

                    SADIE
          We're lost. I need to help my Dad.

                    LISA
          Oh my God, you live in the corn. I
          knew you did, I've been telling
          Chris all along that there are
          people in the corn, but he doesn't
          believe me. Haley's Comet isn't
          coming back anytime soon, so you're
          here to stay, right? Right?
          RIGHT?!

Sadie is uncomfortable, and continues to look back & forth
between the corn and Lisa.

                    LISA (CONT'D)
          We can't make the world a brighter
          place with you in the corn. The
          corn needs to breathe and you're
          choking it. DON'T CHOKE IT!!!!

Lisa grabs Sadie by the shoulders, shakes her.

                    LISA (CONT'D)
          If you choke the corn we can't
          live. I won't let you kill me!

Sadie starts to cry and Lisa grabs her by the throat.

                    LISA (CONT'D)
          I WON'T LET YOU KILL ME!!!

Something's hand reaches out of the corn, grabs the arm that
Lisa is using to choke Sadie and snaps it like a twig. Sadie
falls backwards, she scrambles out of the way as Something
emerges from the corn, and lifts Lisa up off the ground,
looking her eye to eye.

69   EXT. FOREST - DUSK   69

Clayton & Sheriff Collins walk in the distance, when Clayton
spots Jake's cell phone on the ground.

                    CLAYTON
          There!

They run to the cell phone.

                    SHERIFF COLLINS
          It's Jake's!

Sheriff Collins slides the phone on, the voice recording app
is still on. There is a time showing in the corner.

                    SHERIFF COLLINS (CONT'D)
          There's a recording.

Sheriff Collin's plays the recording.

                    MAYOR
          Where is that?

                    SAM
          It's heading to the Devil's Cookie
          Jar.

                    MAYOR
          The gully & cave systems?

                    JAKE
          Tell me Sadie is still...

                                                  CUT TO:

70   EXT. TRAILER - SUNDOWN   70

                    LISA
              (laughing hysterically)

Something clamps down on Lisa's head and bites it, shaking
violently. Lisa's headless body flies across the yard and
smashes against the trailer with a very large THUD. Something
dispenses Lisa's head out of its mouth with a flick of the
tongue, it falls to the ground at Sadie's feet, eyes looking
up at Sadie she looks down at Lisa's dismembered head.

                                                  CUT TO:

71   EXT. FOREST - SUNDOWN   71

Sheriff Collins & Clayton listen to the recording.

                    SAM
          He said to shut up! You best shut
          the fuck up!

A large THUD bellows north of Sheriff Collins & Clayton.
Sheriff Collins shuts off the recording.

                SHERIFF COLLINS
          What was that?

                    CLAYTON
          I don't know, but it was close.

Both take off running toward the embankment. They reach the
top and see the trailer in the distance, and a glimpse of
Something disappears into the tree line behind the trailer.

                SHERIFF COLLINS
          What the hell is that?

Sheriff Collins & Clayton run toward the trailer disappearing
into the cornfield.

72   EXT. DEVIL'S COOKIE JAR - DUSK   72

Swat sets up a high powered DART GUN on a ledge halfway down
the gully wall.

Swat sets a box of darts on the ground, removes one, and
loads it into the dart gun. He takes aim at a log leaf on
the gully floor about 50 yards away, pulls the trigger, and
pins the log leaf to the log with the dart.

Seweryna walks past the leaf log, immediately after dart pins
the leaf, dragging a deer carcass. Once in place, Seweryna
removes the lids of two large BUCKETS marked "Turkey Manure"
and pours both buckets over the deer carcass She turns and
waves both arms in the air towards an embankment of ferns.

                    SEWERYNA
          Lights?

                                              CUT TO:

Vaughn, almost completely obscured by the ferns, watches
Seweryna through a thermal imaging camera. Her temperature
registers bright and waving through the monitor. Vaughn
raises his hand in the air above the ferns and gives a
"thumbs up."

                    VAUGHN
          Camera?

                                        CUT TO:

Swat pulls a monocle over his left eye, through it he can see
the thermal imaging display from Vaughn's location.

                    SWAT
          Action!

                                        CUT TO:

Seweryna loads an identical dart into her hand dart gun, and
holsters it on her hip. She takes a loaded magazine from her
belt and loads it into the handle of her other hand gun
before putting it in the other hip holster. She then places
a deer call up to her mouth and blows into it creating a loud
mating grunt, before attaching it to her belt as well.

                    SEWERYNA
               (into her ear piece)
          Kori?

Kori replies through the ear piece

                    KORI
          Go for Kori.

                    SEWERYNA
          We are set here. What do you have
          on radar?

                    KORI
          Anomalies all over the area.
          Closest one is about 2 miles south
          east of you, but moving very
          slowly, and 2 separate ones
          directly east at about 4 & 4.5
          miles which seem to be moving much
          faster than the S.E., and one of
          them is Sheriff Collins & company.

                    SEWERYNA
          ETA?

                    KORI
          I would say they'll all reach your
          area around the same time, about 45-
          60 minutes from now.

Swat & Vaughn chime in.

                         SWAT
          Sun will be down by then.

                         VAUGHN
          And we'll have eyes in the dark.

Seweryna turns and looks down the gully.

                         SEWERYNA
          T-minus 20 minutes until high
          alert. Humans won't have a better
          way of getting in than through the
          trail leading in, so everyone stay
          silent until the beast is on site.
          Swat will take the shot, Vaughn
          you're on interference if any of
          the humans get in the way.

Seweryna touches her scar momentarily.

                         SEWERYNA (CONT'D)
          No repeats of Norway, please.

73   EXT. TRAILER - DUSK   73

Sheriff Collins emerges from the cornfield with her gun
drawn. She scans the area with the barrel extended, and is
shocked by the head on the ground. She kneels to get a
better look.

                         SHERIFF COLLINS
          Dear God!

Clayton exits the cornfield and stands over Sheriff Collins.

                         CLAYTON
          You know her?

                         SHERIFF COLLINS
          Lisa Evers. Area meth addict.
          Always wanted her to get cleaned
          up.

                         CLAYTON
          Probably a good that she didn't,
          doubt she felt a thing.

Sheriff Collins notices the huge dent on the side of the
trailer, she stands and investigates. Clayton follows. They
find Lisa's body in the tall grass.

                    SHERIFF COLLINS
          How many times did your family
          interact with this thing?

                    CLAYTON
          Not much. Few times over the years.

                    SHERIFF COLLINS
          Never aggressively?

                    CLAYTON
          Not once.

Sheriff Collins scans the area again.

Clayton speaks into the earpiece.

                    CLAYTON (CONT'D)
          Kori, what's directly west of our
          location?

                    KORI
               (over ear piece)
          The containment team.

Sheriff Collins looks into the distance.

                    SHERIFF COLLINS
          The Devil's Cookie Jar.

                    CLAYTON
          Told you they were good.

74   EXT. FOREST - SUNDOWN   74

Sam limps along through the forest followed by Mayor Stanley
& Jake. A river runs close behind them.

                    SAM
          Sun will be down soon. We need to
          start thinking about setting up
          camp.

                    MAYOR
          We can settle in once we get to the
          Devil's Cookie Jar.

                    SAM
          Little more than a mile away.

                    MAYOR
          Then what the hell do you even
          bring it up for?

Sam stops and confronts Mayor Stanley.

                    SAM
          You know, for someone who'd be lost
          and clueless out here without a
          guide, you sure have a strong
          opinion on how shit should go down.

Mayor Stanley, pushes Jake aside, challenges the
confrontation.

                    MAYOR
          And I could have left your ass back
          in Lockridge. I could have brought
          Travis Kennedy, or Clover Buresh,
          with me instead. Neither would
          have whined the whole fucking time
          and moved so God damned slow!

Sam points his rifle and shoots Mayor Stanley in the leg at
point blank range. Mayor Stanley falls to the ground,
screaming.

75   EXT. FOREST - SUNDOWN   75

The shot rings out across the forest. Something stops quickly
and turns toward the noise. Something growls, a snarl
spreads across its face, as it smashes through the forest in
the direction the shot came from.

76   EXT. FOREST - SUNDOWN   76

Sheriff Collins & Clayton stop suddenly after the gunshot.

                    SHERIFF COLLINS
          That was close.

                    CLAYTON
          Wrong direction though.

                    SHERIFF COLLINS
          Jake could be in trouble!

                    CLAYTON
          He's with Sam, he's fine.

Sheriff Collins remembers Jake's phone, she opens it again
and continues playing the recording.

                    SAM
               (through cell phone)
          You & your daughter are not
          supposed to be here! Don't think
          for one second that I won't take
          you out of this equation. Hell, if
          the wildlife doesn't get you, I'll
          be the one who'll head the
          investigation, and what really
          happened will never come to light
          anyway. So just keep testing me!

Sheriff Collins is speechless. Clayton grabs her by the
shoulders and looks her dead in the eye.

                    CLAYTON
          Sadie is out there. We need to
          stay the course and find your
          daughter.

Sheriff Collins shakes her head as she wipes away tears.

                    SHERIFF COLLINS
          And then I'm gonna royally kick
          Sam's ass!

Sheriff Collins storms ahead.

77   EXT. FOREST - SUNDOWN   77

Sam stands above the fallen Mayor. Jake backs away slowly.

                    SAM
          Get the fuck up!

Mayor writhes on the ground, groaning.

                    SAM (CONT'D)
          Let's see how fast you move now,
          Dickhead!

Jake slips away into the forest. Mayor Stanley notices and
fights through the pain.

                    MAYOR
          You...let him...get away.

Mayor Stanley points at Jake running deeper into the woods.
Sam spins to see Jake escaping. He lifts his gun and fires
multiple rounds at Jake.

A heavy rhythmic galloping is heard as Something bursts
through the heavy brush at Sam & the Mayor.

Something knocks Sam away, as it stands above Mayor Stanley and roars a deafening bellow down at him.

Sadie stumbles out of the woods and watches. Sam jumps up and grabs Sadie, who shrieks.

Something spins to face off with Sam and his hostage. Something barks a warning grunt.

Mayor Stanley hops up to his feet behind Something, and raises his rifle at point blank range.

                    SAM
               (yelling to Mayor Stanley)
          SHOOT IT!

Something pounds the ground with both hands and blasts all quills out as wide as possible. One quill flies off and skewers Mayor Stanley through the trachea, pinning him to a tree directly behind him.

Something spins towards the choking noise behind it. Sam pushes Sadie to the ground, raises his rifle and pulls the trigger three times, grazing Something's head and hitting it in the shoulder, until he is out of ammo.

Something dives for cover, spinning around the trunk of a tree with it's palm, and then dives toward Sadie, barrel rolling as it scoops the child up in its chest and then leaps into the river. Something is submerged, with only it's quills sticking above water, as it swiftly makes it's way upstream.

Sam stands, reloads his rifle, checks his GPS, and follows the river which flows directly into the Devil's Cookie Jar.

                    SAM (CONT'D)
          I'm coming for ya!

Sam quickly hobbles away, as the body Mayor Stanley twitches involuntarily behind him.

78   EXT. DEVIL'S COOKIE JAR - NIGHT   78

The gully is quiet, Seweryna & her team are strategically stationed and are motionless. Seweryna is positioned amongst a heavy growth of ferns on the gully floor, watching the deer.

                    SEWERYNA
               (in earpiece)
          Where are they, Kori?

                    KORI
              (through earpiece)
          I've got radar eyes on Sheriff
          Collins & Clayton, coming in from
          the north, they should be reaching
          you any minute.

                    SEWERYNA
          Radio them, they are to stay out of
          the location. Repeat, keep them out
          of the location.

                    KORI
          Then there's smaller anomaly coming
          up slowly from the southeast.
          Should be coming right towards you
          through the gully.

                    SEWERYNA
          How small?

                    KORI
          Man sized.

                    SEWERYNA
          The husband.

Seweryna motions to Vaughn, who comes out of hiding to
reposition himself farther down the gully floor.

                    SEWERYNA (CONT'D)
          Where's our prize?

                    KORI
          That's all I have showing at the
          moment.

                    SEWERYNA
          What do you mean? Where is it?

                    KORI
          I don't know, it's not been on
          radar for a while now.

79   EXT. FOREST - NIGHT   79

     Sheriff Collins & Clayton trudge through the forest. Kori
     talks over the radio.

                    KORI
          Base to Sheriff Collins...

     They stop moving to reply.

                    SHERIFF COLLINS
          Go for Collins...

                    KORI
          Direct orders from Seweryna, DO NOT
          enter the gully. Element of
          surprise is compromised with a
          heavier population.

                    SHERIFF COLLINS
          Bullshit! We're coming in!
          That's...

Clayton interrupts, responding to Kori.

                    CLAYTON
          We got it Kori, we'll hang tight
          until further direction. Over.

Sheriff Collins reacts to Clayton's submission.

                    SHERIFF COLLINS
          What the fuck?

Clayton switches off his ear piece. He reaches up and takes
Sheriff Collins' ear piece as well and shuts it off.

                    CLAYTON
          We're going in military style now.
          Follow me.

Clayton gets low and moves slowly through the underbrush.
Sheriff Collins follows.

80   EXT. DEVIL'S COOKIE JAR - NIGHT   80

Swat takes aim at the bait deer from his ledge. The Flir
image from his monocle shows very little heat signature, and
no movement at all. In the distance, a yellowish blip
appears on the screen and moves farther back in the gully
away from the deer.

                    SWAT
              (whispering)
          Husband approaching.

                    VAUGHN
              (whispering)
          Had him in sight about 15 seconds
          ago. Will intercept.

81   EXT. DEVIL'S COOKIE JAR FLOOR - NIGHT   81

Sam limps along the gully floor, struggling to move in the
moonlight with a bad leg and a debris riddled trail.

Sam stops and leans against a large rock for a moment, rifle
in hand. He searches the area, trying to make out anything
in the dark. A hand reaches down from the top of the rock
and covers Sam's mouth.

Sam reacts by raising his rifle, which is grabbed with
another hand from atop the rock. Vaughn pries the rifle from
Sam's grasp.

                    VAUGHN
               (whispering)
          Quiet...we're with Clayton and your
          wife.

Sam thinks quickly and nods in agreement.

                    VAUGHN (CONT'D)
          Follow me.

Vaughn slides off the rock without making a sound. He hands
the rifle back to Sam and scurries along the gully floor as
Sam tries his best to keep up.

Vaughn reaches his vantage point and helps Sam fall in behind
him. Vaughn hands Sam his rifle again, as Sam slinks against
the hill behind him.

                    VAUGHN (CONT'D)
               (whispering into ear
                piece)
          Husband is secured, awaiting
          target.

82   EXT. RIVER BANK - NIGHT   82

Sadie wades out of the water onto the river bank. Something
slips out of the water and shakes itself off like a dog.
Ahead of them both, in the moonlight, is the entrance to the
Devil's Cookie Jar. Something eyes the area closely, and
begins to purr at its familiar sight.

Something sniffs the air a couple of times, and looks
confused. It takes a long nasal inhale as it sways its head
from side to side, and then ultimately points into the gully.

Something's purr turns into a low growl and it begins to
stalk into the mouth of the gully crouched low. Sadie
follows.

83   EXT. SHERIFF COLLINS HOME - NIGHT   83

            Kori sits watching the radar. Suddenly, a new entity appears
            on the screen. Each wave of the radar screen beeps with
            every pass.

                              KORI
                        (into the ear piece)
                    I think Elvis is in the building.
                    Heading your way about 60 yards
                    out.

84   EXT. DEVIL'S COOKIE JAR - NIGHT   84

            Swat responds.

                              SWAT
                    I need eyes, Vaughn.

85   EXT. DEVIL'S COOKIE JAR FLOOR - NIGHT   85

            Vaughn zooms in, further down the gully. A distant & broad
            heat signature appears.

                              VAUGHN
                    I've got an Elvis sighting. Coming
                    in slowly.

86   EXT. DEVIL'S COOKIE JAR - NIGHT   86

            Swat's face lights up from the glow of the heat signature
            projecting through his monocle.

                              SWAT
                    Target acquired. Locked & loaded,
                    awaiting cue.

            Seweryna interrupts over the ear piece.

                              SEWERYNA
                    Tranq's only, we're taking Elvis
                    alive.

87   EXT. DEVIL'S COOKIE JAR FLOOR - NIGHT   87

            Vaughn replies.

                              VAUGHN
                    Roger that!

Vaughn zooms in on the Flir, he notices a second heat
signature trailing behind Something. Vaughn turns to Sam and
nudges him, points to the screen. Sam leans forward to see
Sadie's figure walking along with the beast.

                    VAUGHN (CONT'D)
          Your daughter.

Sam nods his head again. Vaughn replies into the ear piece.

                    VAUGHN (CONT'D)
          Sheriff's daughter is in the line
          of fire. I repeat, the Sheriff's
          daughter is in the line of fire.

88   EXT. DEVIL'S COOKIE JAR - NIGHT   88

Swat is stoic and focused, regardless of the news.

                    SWAT
          Can you isolate the child to clear
          the shot?

89   EXT. DEVIL'S COOKIE JAR FLOOR - NIGHT   89

Vaughn surveys the area for a new vantage possibility.

                    VAUGHN
          Will be tough, but if Seweryna can
          lay down a suppressing fire to
          distract Elvis, I think I can
          intercept long enough for you to
          get the shot.

Seweryna responds over ear piece.

                    SEWERYNA
          No firing, flash grenade at 45
          degrees south of target.

90   EXT. DEVIL'S COOKIE JAR - NIGHT   90

Sheriff Collins & Clayton crawl through the brush and peer
over the ledge into the gully. Occasionally, the sound of
rustling can be heard, but they can see no movement.

                    SHERIFF COLLINS
          Where is everyone?

> CLAYTON
> It's an ambush, likely triangular
> crossfire.

Clayton points down into the gully almost directly below them. Sheriff Collins looks hard. Out of the darkness she sees a fern shift slightly.

> CLAYTON (CONT'D)
> That would put the other two there,
> and there.

Clayton points to the outcropping where Swat is positioned, but out of sight, and the rocky inlet where Seweryna is stationed & also out of sight. Sheriff Collins nods, as they both watch intently.

91   EXT. DEVIL'S COOKIE JAR FLOOR - NIGHT   91

The gully entrance is a deep black trail, with slivers of moonlight slicing through the canopy in a few open sections.

Something emerges slowly out of the darkness and passes through the moonlight cautiously. Sadie trots alongside toward its hind legs.

Once in the darkness again, its eye shine illuminates the trail bobbing up and down with each step it takes before revealing itself in the next sliver of moonlight.

92   EXT. DEVIL'S COOKIE JAR - NIGHT   92

Sweat rolls down the side of Swat's face.

> SWAT
> (whispering into the ear
> piece)
> 10 yards away from intercept.

93   EXT. DEVIL'S COOKIE JAR FLOOR - NIGHT   93

Something darts out of the moonlight and into the darkness again, then stops. It scans the gully, smelling the air. Something looks up at Swat's position, inhales deeply, lowers its quills, and growls at the ledge.

94   EXT. DEVIL'S COOKIE JAR - NIGHT   94

Swat clenches his jaw.

> SWAT
> It knows we're here. I have a
> shot.

Seweryna replies over the ear piece.

> SEWERYNA
> Negative. Initiating intercept in
> 10, 9, 8,...

95   EXT. DEVIL'S COOKIE JAR FLOOR - NIGHT   95

Vaughn moves into position to intercept Sadie with
Something's attention on Swat's position.

                                                  CUT TO:

Seweryna prepares a flash grenade, reels back to throw it as
she continues to count.

> SEWERYNA
> 7, 6, 5,

96   EXT. DEVIL'S COOKIE JAR - NIGHT   96

Sheriff Collins watches Vaughn position himself, while Sadie
looks up in the same direction as Something. Sheriff Collins
covers her mouth with her hand.

Suddenly Sam leans forward from behind Vaughn, revealing
himself in the moonlight.

> SHERIFF COLLINS
> Oh my God...

97   EXT. DEVIL'S COOKIE JAR FLOOR - NIGHT   97

Vaughn anticipates his attack.

> SEWERYNA
> (whispering over ear
> piece)
> 4, 3, 2...

Sam leans forward, with his rifle inches away from the back
of Vaughn's head and pulls the trigger before Seweryna can
reach the countdown.

Vaughn crumbles down the hill, out of the cover of the ferns.
Sam sinks back into the darkness.

Something spins wildly toward the hill and roars. Vaughn
rolls to the gully floor at its feet.

                                                  CUT TO:

With Something's attention redirected, Seweryna spins to the
opposite side of the rock cover. She reels back to throw the
flash grenade, as Something clamps onto Vaughn's body with
it's mouth and throws it into the air at Swat's location.
She throws the grenade.

98   EXT. DEVIL'S COOKIE JAR - NIGHT   98

Vaughn's body flies through the air at Swat, who quickly
rolls with his rifle and repositions himself without
hesitation or distraction. Vaughn's body lands next to Swat
on the ledge, Swat is steadfast with his focus on the
creature below.

99   EXT. DEVIL'S COOKIE JAR FLOOR - NIGHT   99

Flash grenade lands with a huge boom next to Something, a
burst of light illuminates the gully floor. Something leaps
away from the location, as Sadie is knocked back by the
impact.

Sam jumps up from hiding and sprays bullets wildly at
Something. The beast rolls into the same rocky cover that
Seweryna has taken cover behind.

Seweryna dives out of the way of Something, scrambles along
the other side of the rocks, out of sight from Something.

Sam hops down the hillside and pulls Sadie up. He turns to
face everyone with the rifle, and Sadie directly in front of
him as a human shield. Sam spies quills rising above the
rocks just before Seweryna scurries around the corner on the
other side.

100   EXT. DEVIL'S COOKIE JAR - NIGHT   100

Clayton slings himself over the edge of the cliff feet first,
scurrying down the side of the hill before leaping off and
falling directly on top of Sam.

                                                  CUT TO:

Swat redirects aim towards Seweryna. His vision of Something
is blocked by the rocks.

                    SWAT
              (into the ear piece)
          No shot.

101   EXT. DEVIL'S COOKIE JAR FLOOR - NIGHT   101

       Seweryna spies Sam taking aim at her, and kicks herself up
       just as Clayton lands on top of Sam and toppling him to the
       ground.

       Seweryna sprints to Sadie, behind her Something crawls on top
       of the rocks and roars loudly, swaying its head.

       A dart flies through the air and misses Something's neck by
       an inch, bouncing off the rocks. Something's attention is
       pulled back to Swat's position.

       Seweryna dives and pulls Sadie down into the ferns. They
       disappear out of sight.

       Sam pulls himself up, Clayton lays on the ground. His leg
       broken from the fall.

                    SAM
          Jesus Christ, Clayton!

       Clayton pulls himself up and turns to get away. Sam kicks
       him in the back and Clayton, unable to use his fractured leg,
       stumbles and falls forward against the rocks next to
       Something. Clayton leans against the rocks and turns to face
       Sam.

       Sam raises his rifle and points it directly at Clayton.

                    SAM (CONT'D)
          Thank you for your service, War
          Hero...

102   EXT. DEVIL'S COOKIE JAR - NIGHT   102

       Sheriff Collins takes aim at Sam from high above, and fires.

103   EXT. DEVIL'S COOKIE JAR FLOOR - NIGHT   103

       Something leans down and bites Clayton on the shoulder &
       neck, pulling him over the rocks out of the line of fire.

       Sam is hit in the back by Sheriff Collins' bullet. He drops
       to his knees and turns to see Sheriff Collins above, smoking
       gun in hand.

> SAM
> Fuckin' bitch...

CUT TO:

Behind the rocks, Something releases Clayton who drops to the
ground, bleeding severely from the neck wound. Something
nuzzles Clayton with its snout, but Clayton slips away
quickly and takes his last breath.

Something raises & lowers its quills repeatedly, first slowly
and then picking up speed. The air noise "whooshes" loudly
throughout the gully.

CUT TO:

In the ferns, Sadie lays unconscious, as Seweryna stays out
of sight.

CUT TO:

104   EXT. DEVIL'S COOKIE JAR - NIGHT   104

Sheriff Collins runs along the top ledge of the Cookie Jar.
Along the other side, Swat reloads.

CUT TO:

Swat reloads a new dart.

> SWAT
> Elvis is all shook up! Do you have
> a shot?

Seweryna replies via ear piece.

> SEWERYNA
> Negative.

Swat peers through his monocle, the rocks are cold as
Something's quills rise and fall behind them.

> SWAT
> I've still got eyes on the stage,
> waiting on the encore.

Suddenly the quills stop, laying down & out of sight. The
rocks remain still & silent.

CUT TO:

105   EXT. SHERIFF COLLINS HOME - NIGHT   105

Kori watches the IST screen as a giant blip disappears. Kori
taps on the screen.

                    KORI
          Ummm, there's a problem. Elvis is
          wearing Blue Suede Shoes.

106   EXT. DEVIL'S COOKIE JAR FLOOR - NIGHT   106

Seweryna holds her breath, and listens. Something is
stirring behind the rocks, rhythmic thuds echo throughout the
gully.

                    SEWERYNA
          What's it doing?

Swat answers through the ear piece.

                    SWAT
          Not sure. Still no eyes on it.

Seweryna speaks into the ear piece.

                    SEWERYNA
          Kori?

107   EXT. SHERIFF COLLINS HOME - NIGHT   107

Kori unplugs the IST screen, and then plugs it back in.

                    KORI
          The signal just disappeared. I
          think Elvis has left the building.

108   EXT. DEVIL'S COOKIE JAR FLOOR - NIGHT   108

Seweryna glances up at Swat who doesn't flinch.

                    SEWERYNA
               (to Kori)
          Elvis has not left the building, I
          can still hear it.

Swat replies through the ear piece.

                    SWAT
          Going to need a repeat of Norway.

                    SEWERYNA
          Damn it, not again!

                    SWAT
            (through the ear piece)
          Isn't my fault this time!

Seweryna emerges from the ferns. She raises her gun, checks
for a dart, takes a deep breath and explodes in a dead sprint
to the rocks. She baseball slides on her hip from the front
of the rocks to the back with gun aimed. There is nothing
behind the rocks.

                    SEWERYNA
          Nothing! Elvis HAS left the
          building.

109   EXT. DEVIL'S COOKIE JAR - NIGHT   109

Swat finally relaxes his focus, and removes his monocle.

                    SWAT
          Son of a bitch! It lowered it's
          body temperature.

Swat quickly looks around the gully, trying to get a visual.
He stands, and lights a flare.

CRACK!

In the glow behind Swat, a set of quills shoots straight up.
A quill flies off of Something's back as it clings to the
rocky wall of the gully. The quill lodges in Swat's shoulder,
he spins quickly from the impact to face Something.

Something backhands Swat in the chest and sends him flying
off the ledge.

110   EXT. DEVIL'S COOKIE JAR FLOOR - NIGHT   110

Swat flies from the ledge, his body limp and cart-wheeling,
he lands on his back with a thud.

Seweryna sprints from the rocks to Swat's side.

Above them, Something climbs off the wall onto the ledge and
roars in the moonlight.

111   EXT. DEVIL'S COOKIE JAR - NIGHT   111

Sheriff Collins races along the top of the gully, looking for
a way to climb down. She finds an incline that isn't as
steep, and looks for a spot to descend.

Something appears out of the woods and walks up behind
Sheriff Collins, grabs her from behind.

Sheriff Collins screams as slips and falls over the edge.
She grabs hold of a jagged rock and holds on. Something
leans over the edge of the gully and looks down at Sheriff
Collins. It's Jake.

                    SHERIFF COLLINS
          JAKE!

Jake reaches out to Sheriff Collins. She takes his hand and
he hauls her back up. They embrace. Jake holds out his
hands.

                    JAKE
          Can you take these off?

Sheriff Collins unlocks the cuffs on Jake's hands.

                    SHERIFF COLLINS
          Sam did this?

                    JAKE
          Yeah, he's lost it. Have you found
          Sadie?

                    SHERIFF COLLINS
          She's down there.

They both react to the bellowing roar from Something.

                    JAKE
          C'mon. Let's go.

Jake secures his footing off the side of the incline and
offers his hand to Sheriff Collins to help. She ignores it
and scrambles down the side of the incline on her own.

                    JAKE (CONT'D)
          God, I love that woman!

Jake follows behind Sheriff Collins.

112   EXT. DEVIL'S COOKIE JAR - NIGHT   112

     Something finishes its roar on the ledge. It leans down and
     sniffs Vaughn's body, nudges it with it's tusks. Vaughn is
     lifeless, Something steps on Vaughn and pulls him backward
     out of the way. Something looks down into the gully at
     Seweryna & Swat, it growls and climbs over the side of the
     ledge.

113   EXT. DEVIL'S COOKIE JAR FLOOR - NIGHT   113

     Something scales down the side of the gully wall above
     Seweryna & Swat. Seweryna tries to lift Swat up, he groans
     in pain.

                         SEWERYNA
               It's coming for us. We gotta move.

                         SWAT
               I can't feel my legs.

     Seweryna looks around for anything, Something reaches the
     gully floor and stares her down.

                         SEWERYNA
               Still not as bad as Norway!

                         SWAT
               Yet.

     Something sneers and growls deeply.

     Seweryna draws a long survival knife from the back of her
     belt and kneels over Swat ready to defend them both. Swat
     turns his head away.

                         SWAT (CONT'D)
               Seweryna...

                         SEWERYNA
               What?

                         SWAT
               Behind you.

     A gunshot rings out, Swat is hit in the head. Seweryna turns
     and falls backward, Sam stands above her, bloody and
     disheveled. He points the gun directly at Seweryna.

                         SAM
               I don't know who the hell you are,
               but I am done fucking around.

Sam shuffles forward, Seweryna scoots backward. Something barks its displeasure, drawing Sam's attention.

                    SEWERYNA
          You'll never get away from it.

Sam shoots Seweryna in the leg. She screams in pain.

                    SAM
          Now you won't either.

Something sulks low to the ground, like a cat ready to pounce. It moves forward toward Sam slowly, circling them and rattling its quills in a defiant warning. Sam shambles past Seweryna and points his gun at the monster.

                    SAM (CONT'D)
          C'mon you motherfucker! C'MON!!

Seweryna pulls herself up behind Sam and buries her knife deep into his back. Sam's eyes widen from the pain. Sam stumbles backward and knocks Seweryna to the ground again.

Sheriff Collins & Jake reach the scene at full sprint. Sam shifts his body around, knife in his back, and stands over Seweryna.

                    SAM (CONT'D)
          I should have killed you the first
          time.

Sam points the gun at Seweryna.

                    SHERIFF COLLINS
     SAM!

Sam looks over at Sheriff Collins. Sheriff Collins draws her gun at Sam.

                    SHERIFF COLLINS (CONT'D)
          You're fired!

She shoots Sam in the throat. Blood gushes out and Sam falls dead.

Seweryna pulls her knife from Sam's back and scrambles along the floor of the gully towards Sheriff Collins & Jake.

Something approaches Sam. It clamps down on Sam's back with its mouth and rips a large chunk of flesh off. Something proceeds to eat at Sam's body.

Sadie emerges from the ferns, crying. Jake runs to her side as Sheriff Collins helps Seweryna to her feet.

They watch Something finish its meal and casually walk over
to Sadie & Jake. It nuzzles Sadie, who stops crying and lays
her hand tenderly on Something's muzzle.

                    SEWERYNA
          I told you it would find its way
          home.

Sheriff Collins & Seweryna make their way toward Jake &
Sadie.

                    SHERIFF COLLINS
          Not yet, it hasn't.

They all gather around Sadie and embrace. Something purrs its
approval.

                                        FADE OUT.

                                        FADE IN:

114   EXT. SHERIFF COLLINS HOME - DUSK   114

        Sun is setting on the horizon, Sheriff Collins' cruiser sits
        in the driveway. The light in Sadie's room turns on.

115   INT. SADIE'S ROOM - NIGHT   115

        Jake finishes reading a story to Sadie and closes the book.

                    JAKE
          Time for bed princess.

        Jake tucks Sadie into bed, and gives her a peck on the head.

                    JAKE (CONT'D)
          Good night, Kiddo.

                    SADIE
          Good night, Daddy. I love you.

                    JAKE
          I love you too.

        Jake turns to leave the room.

                    JAKE (CONT'D)
          And no getting out of bed.

        Sadie grins widely.

                         JAKE (CONT'D)
          I mean it.

Jake turns out the light and shuts the door. Sadie lies in
bed, the light of the moon shining through the window. A
shadow washes over her face.

A single enormous hand is open and gently pressed against the
outside of the window. Sadie smiles, sits up, and pulls back
the covers.

                                        FADE TO BLACK.

www.ingramcontent.com/pod-product-compliance
Lightning Source LLC
Chambersburg PA
CBHW050554160726
48003CB00002B/884